A Candlelight Ecstasy Romance®

"YOU'RE NOT GOING ANYWHERE," FLYNN TOLD HER QUIETLY, "UNTIL I START GETTING SOME ANSWERS."

Brittany shook her head. "There's nothing to say. You were right before. I was after your money. I showed up in Costa del Sol to try to catch your eye." She cast a glance in his direction, smiling with no humor. "I really don't think you're worth it after all. So if you'll just drive me back—"

Her voice died along with her smile. He didn't blink, he just stared at her, ruthless, cold, totally hard.

"You're not who you say you are," he began. "And I've changed my mind—you're definitely not after my money. But you are after something, and you want it so badly that you were willing to make love with me to get it." His eyes glittered dangerously. "Just what *are* you after?"

CANDLELIGHT ECSTASY CLASSIC ROMANCES

SIREN FROM THE SEA

Heather Graham

A CANDLELIGHT ECSTASY ROMANCE®

Published by
Dell Publishing Co., Inc.
1 Dag Hammarskjold Plaza
New York, New York 10017

Dell ® TM 681510, Dell Publishing Co., Inc.

Candlelight Ecstasy Romance®, 1,203,540, is a registered trademark of Dell Publishing Co., Inc., New York, New York.

ISBN: 0-440-18057-0

Printed in the United States of America

June 1987

10 9 8 7 6 5 4 3 2 1

WFH

To Our Readers:

We have been delighted with your enthusiastic response to Candlelight Ecstasy Romances®, and we thank you for the interest you have shown in this exciting series.

In the upcoming months we will continue to present the distinctive sensuous love stories you have come to expect only from Ecstasy. We look forward to bringing you many more books from your favorite authors and also the very finest work from new authors of contemporary romantic fiction.

As always, we are striving to present the unique, absorbing love stories that you enjoy most—books that are more than ordinary romance. Your suggestions and comments are always welcome. Please write to us at the address below.

Sincerely,

The Editors
Candlelight Romances
1 Dag Hammarskjold Plaza
New York, New York 10017

SIREN FROM
THE SEA

PROLOGUE

She was a lone figure, small but straight and dignified. In honor of Alice she was dressed in black; the only color about her was the beautiful auburn of her hair, a streak of sunset beneath the black of her hat and veil.

Ashes to ashes, dust to dust . . .

She wasn't going to cry. She had promised herself that she wasn't going to cry again. Alice certainly wouldn't want her to do that.

But she felt so alone.

She had just lost her last living blood relation and the birds were still singing and the sun was actually shining . . .

She turned and walked away. Blindly, she almost stumbled. Someone caught her hand, and she turned to see the kindly eyes of Inspector Brice Holden.

"Miss Martin—"

"I'm fine," she promised softly, but he insisted on seeing her back to her aunt's flat, and promised again that he would do everything in his power.

But a month later, Brittany Martin still lingered in London, and nothing had been done. She kept calling back home, back to the beach, and asking that they extend her leave of absence. She'd worked for the state for a long time and she knew that she was one of the best lifeguards on the beach—

but she was still pushing her luck. They wouldn't hold her job forever. But she didn't really care. She couldn't leave, she couldn't go home, she couldn't pick up her life again. She had to wait, she had to know that the man would be brought to justice. For the hundredth time, she picked up the phone and called the inspector.

"Brittany?" Brice Hopkins answered her query.

"Yes, Brice. I want to know if you've got anything yet."

A long sigh was her answer, then, "Brittany, you know that I would do anything in the world for you. And you know how very sorry I am. I cared for Alice deeply."

"But you've got nothing."

"Not quite." Brice hesitated. "I'm pretty sure our man has flown, Brittany. We can't touch him."

Brittany frowned. "What do you mean—you can't touch him?"

"Brittany—whoever this man is, he's cleared out. British fugitives have a habit of disappearing. Usually to the Costa del Sol." He hesitated. "One of your aunt's necklaces appeared in a shop there. Pawned. So we're certain our man has several fences down there, we're equally certain that he's living in a decent style down there. We've been watching the activities of several men. Men with established residences there, too. Who come in, strike, flee quickly. You see, we have no extradition agreement with Spain."

Brittany felt a chill settle over her.

"You mean he may get off scot-free?" she inquired incredulously.

"I'm afraid so."

Brice kept talking, then he hung up. Brittany must have given him some kind of reply, she couldn't remember.

She spent the night tossing and turning, and in the morning she went into the police station. Brice's assistant was a very

10

young man who was easily charmed, and Brittany talked to him for a long time, hoping to glean some information that Brice might be holding from her.

When she was about to give up, the young man was suddenly called out of the room, and while he was gone, another officer came in. He smiled, she smiled. He dropped the papers he was carrying and Brittany quickly bent to help him collect the sheets.

The papers were listings. Listings of British nationals who had come in from the Costa del Sol on the same date that her aunt had died. Men who had departed swiftly, immediately after.

The second was a listing of British nationals living in Costa del Sol whose incomes were questionable. Men who might be having financial trouble. Men who simply didn't explain on paper exactly where they procured all their money . . .

The officer left the papers on the desk and Brittany studied them thoroughly after he'd gone. She memorized the names that appeared on both lists then she fled. As soon as she returned to the flat, she wrote the names down.

And she started wondering about how to go to Spain. As a regular, economy-class tourist? Oh, never! The thought was so ludicrous that she laughed out loud. She would never be given the time of day. These men were the jet set. They moved in society circles, they reeked of money and of all the things that money could buy.

She sat back in the overstuffed armchair beside the hearth and sipped her tea, staring idly at the newspaper she had dropped.

And then she wasn't staring so idly, because the paper seemed to be mocking her thoughts in black and white print.

. . . Costa del Sol . . .

Brittany grabbed the paper. It was an article on a man named Colby. Flynn Colby.

She scanned the picture first. The man had been caught by the photographer while deplaning from a small twin-engine jet. He was a striking individual: dark-haired, tall and straight —handsome features severe with annoyance at the interruption. But if he smiled . . . if that rugged sense of steely determination about his features was gone, he could be charming.

And someone very charming had conned Aunt Alice. Out of her life's savings, her jewelry—even her silver. Perhaps twenty thousand pounds in all. Not a vast fortune—but a life's savings for Alice. Put enough of those life's savings together, and it did become a vast fortune.

Money didn't matter; silver didn't matter. Jewels didn't matter; they were just things.

Alice mattered.

Alice was no longer alive. No longer smiling, laughing, baking wonderful things, spouting off against the Prime Minister or demanding to know from Brittany just what the American president was up to. She was no longer keen and bright and beautiful. No longer—here.

Don't! Brittany warned herself fiercely. It could still make her cry. It was much, much better to be furious. Furious, and determined that something must be done.

She sighed.

Flynn Colby was wealthy. He wouldn't need to steal money from elderly ladies.

All the suspects were wealthy! she reminded herself. Horribly, disgustingly wealthy. And one of them was staying wealthy by stealing from elderly ladies.

Flynn Colby. She had seen the name before, even before today. She had seen write-ups on him before. Once, when he

12

had been dating a Swedish film star. Once when he had won the cup in a yacht race outside of New York City. He was rich; he moved around the world like the wind . . .

She quickly began to read this article. It didn't say much. Just that Flynn Colby had been in London for "business purposes" and was intending to spend the summer at his home in Spain.

At Costa del Sol.

And it mentioned his passion for yachting.

Brittany continued looking through the paper. On the society page she learned that an Ian Drury of London had also been in town for a gala event; he had just returned to his summer home at Costa del Sol.

And on the business page, she discovered that a Joshua Jones, of Hampstead Court, was opening a new office for his import firm—

At Costa del Sol.

Three names. Three names that had been on the lists in the police station.

She closed her eyes. It was insane. The only way to reach these people would be to arrive as jet setter as they were themselves, and she couldn't do that. She hadn't the money and she didn't know a thing about what the "filthy rich" really did. She could never feign money or wealth; it was impossible.

It would be absurd and dangerous.

Go home, Brice had told her over and over again. Go home, and forget. But how could she forget such a thing? If the police could do nothing, someone had to.

The paper was on the floor. She stared at the back with tears fogging her eyes again and then she paused, because again *Costa del Sol* jumped out at her.

She grabbed the paper and began to read the article. "Modern-day Pirate Plagues the Coast of Southern Spain; Sea-robbers Harass Costa del Sol."

It was a warning to British citizens who might be planning a trip to Spain's playground. It was brief, and Brittany wasn't sure why she read it, reread it, and reread it again. And somewhere within it all, her plan was born. A frightening plan, a foolhardy plan—but the only one she could come up with. She told herself that it was ridiculous and dangerous, but then again, she knew that she could take to the sea, that she could swim like a fish . . . That she could feign anything in the water.

She shivered and tossed and turned all night and in the morning she was still shivering.

"You can't do it!" she wearily told her mirror image.

"You have to try," it pleaded in return. "It's a God-given opportunity. It will be easy. It will explain why you haven't any money, it will bring you close to one of them. It can cast you into their social sphere. It's the only way."

"It's insane. I can't pretend to be rich."

"You have to try . . ."

"You haven't the charm to con a man like that. Like Flynn Colby. He'll see through you in the first second. You are no debutante, Brittany Martin!" She continued to argue with herself.

"You can fake it. You have to fake it! He is the one! The one with the passion for yachting. And he's young, and surely, you do know how to flirt!"

It was a wild, absurd scheme. It was the only one that she had! Alice was dead. Brittany didn't want revenge; she wanted justice. She could not forget.

Insane or not, she had to play her dangerous game. She had lost her last relative in the entire world to a careless swindler and no one would help her . . .

"You can't . . ." her common sense argued.

"You have to . . ." her heart answered.

And she knew that she would. There was simply no other way.

CHAPTER ONE

He paused in his labors with the rigging and stared southeasterly, smiling, feet apart, and hands upon his hips. He was a young man, but one who had lived all his years fully, and betrayed that character in the set of his jaw, and in the faint web of lines about his eyes that appeared when he laughed. His eyes, scanning the water, were the type that gave away nothing; and yet there was a shrewdness, an astuteness, about them that might warn the observant that he saw everything. Behind those eyes was a mind that worked ceaselessly; bright, as sharp as a whip, and as finely honed as a seaman's body, accustomed to action. His face was an interesting one, riveting, nicely featured—but his attraction was not so much in his looks, but rather in his movement, or even the lack thereof. Even in repose, he seemed exceptionally alive; energy spun about him like the heat waves spun from the sun.

At the moment, though, he wasn't thinking about action— of any kind. There had just been something about the view that had called him; nature held him there in a bit of awe. He had been called by her tune as any man might, and he felt a touch of magic in the view.

It was a beautiful day: warm and balmy, but touched by breezes. The ocean was at its shimmering best. To the south and the east, deeper waters were gleaming indigo against the clear horizon; here, the indigo paled to turquoise and green—glittering, dancing, filling the senses with the varying mood of the sea. Salt clean and fresh, fantastic beneath the sun. The sun—yes, today was one of those occasions that gave credence to the land mass behind them. Costa del Sol; coast of the sun. Today belonged to the sea, and to the golden orb of the fiery sun. To Neptune, and to all the various gods of the seas.

"Flynn! What are you doing?"

He turned about with a dry grimace. "I'm not real sure. Daydreaming, I think. Fantasizing."

Juan Perez—his best friend and first mate aboard the *Bella Christa*—shook his head and swore lightly in his native Castilian Spanish. "Fantasizing, *amigo?* Most men would say that you live a fantasy. You don't need to fantasize, especially when you are supposed to be pulling in the mainsail."

Flynn laughed and returned to his task of securing the rigging. The mainsail flew and whipped in the breeze, then obediently pulled in and became tight, stretched full by the wind.

"So—you were fantasizing. I thought we came out to discuss business."

"We did—but the afternoon is long. I brought along a book, too." He shrugged. "Something about the sea just attracted me. Don't you ever feel that, Juan?"

"With you—not usually. Usually, I am just worried about cruising through it."

"Well, we're in no hurry now."

"No, but then I am more accustomed to our sea and to our sun. I am a Spaniard. We accept legend and mystery—you English are often too upright, *amigo*, for that which we easily accept."

Flynn was not offended; he laughed. "I'm not English, Juan. I'm Scottish."

Juan waved a hand, clearly stating that to a Spaniard, there was little difference. "All the same," Juan muttered.

Tell that to the Scots, or the English, Flynn thought, but he said nothing. It would be a useless argument with the Spaniard.

"Now the Irish—they are a bit different," Juan was saying. "They have life; fiery tempers—not so cold, eh? But that, I believe, is because of the Spaniards. So many of our ships wrecked upon their shores in the days of the Armada—they have Latin blood in their veins!"

"Watch it, Juan," Flynn said with amusement. "You're setting down stereotypes, and that can be dangerous. I know any number of even-tempered Irish."

"That's because of the English invasions," Juan scoffed. "Temper, Flynn, temper is the spice of life."

"Spice, eh?" Flynn queried. "And what happens when that 'spice of life' flies out of control?"

"It does not—in a gentleman."

"Oh." Flynn grinned. "I see. I get to be 'cold'—but you, a Spaniard, get to be a 'gentleman.' "

"Something like that," Juan agreed with a wide, white smile cutting across his dark, mustachioed, and handsome face.

But then Juan sobered. "I worry about you sometimes, *amigo.*"

"Why is that?"

"Because you are perhaps too controlled—or too much the gentleman, whichever you would prefer. I watch you when you are angry, and you give little sign. It is frightening."

Flynn threw up his hands in exasperation. "And what would you have me do? I can't fly off the handle, Juan. I have to keep a level head. It's imperative that I do in my position, and you know it."

Juan shrugged, unruffled by the heat and tension in the question. Slowly, he smiled again.

"Business is one thing. Life is another." He nodded slowly, as if savoring great wisdom. "Maybe today is good. It's good that you stare out at the sea—and fantasize. And it's good that your voice grows hard with irritation with me—I am your friend. As I said, 'business' is not living. Emotion is living!" He laughed suddenly. "Now Americans . . . I like Americans. They tend to be a bit loco, you know? They plunge in feet first and then they think. But they know how to live, yes. I like Americans."

"Well, I'm glad you like Americans, but you're stereotyping again," Flynn advised.

"Maybe," Juan said, shrugging with dismissal. He grinned. "What was this fantasy I interrupted? Were you expecting Neptune to rise from the sea, trident in hand?"

"Spaniards," Flynn commented, "are crazy as hell."

"You're stereotyping."

"Yeah, I know."

"No Neptune, then, eh?"

Flynn shook his head, a slight smile curving one corner of his lip ruefully. "No. I was just looking at the water and at the sun and thinking that it's one of the most beautiful days I've ever seen. And that your coast is aptly named. And—" Flynn held up a hand when Juan would have interrupted him. "—I was thinking that it was easy to see why our ancestors could believe in serpents and sea gods and nymphs and the like."

"Mermaids," Juan said.

"Why not?" Flynn grinned. "Sounds like fun to me." He turned around and started for the bow, calling over his shoulder, "I'm going up to the bow to tighten the jenny. We can have drinks and lunch then, and figure out our strategy for the next week or so."

Juan nodded. Flynn continued onward to the bow, neatly stepping around the rigging. Juan—one of the best sailors he knew—began to roll the hemp line about the mainmast to his liking. Juan, he knew, was almost as incapable as he of sitting still. If there was something to be done, Juan was going to do it.

Maybe that was what made them such good friends, Flynn mused. They were close in age, but more than that, they were both . . . restless. They liked to move. They liked to come and go as they chose, and yet they also shared a sense of duty. He shook his head. "You are crazy, *amigo*," Flynn muttered to himself. "I get as hot as the next man—I'm just aware that throwing things will never change a situation."

And, he reminded himself, springing forward and grabbing the proper line, I just can't afford to lose my cool when decisions have to be made.

"Hey, Flynn!"

Flynn paused, turning toward the bow, curious at the tone of Juan's voice.

Juan continued then, his voice still carrying that strange tone.

"Do you really believe in mermaids?"

Flynn arched a curious brow at his friend. He dropped the length of the jenny line he had been holding and hurried from the bow to stand beside Juan, who was now frowning and narrowing his eyes against the sun's glaze to stare out at the mildly rippling, azure water.

"Have I truly gone loco, *amigo*, or is that a woman—"

"It *is* a woman!" Flynn interrupted incredulously. "In trouble," he muttered, hopping to the bow rail with swift grace and plunging into the sea with a smooth dive. He struck the water and immediately began to swim with strong strokes, his

21

sun-browned and sinewed body cleanly and effortlessly propelled toward his destination . . . the girl.

At first glance, she might have been a sun worshipper, stretched out to catch the midmorning rays, her sleek form every bit as enticing as ever an advertisement for sun lotion. But after the first start of seeing such a beauty drift by as if cast up by mischievous Neptune, it became apparent that she was drifting on what could barely be called a plank, and that an arm drifted lazily in the water because the mysterious beauty was barely conscious . . . if she was conscious at all.

Flynn reached the plank and grasped it. She started, and her eyes opened, wide . . . frightened. They were green. Deep green, rich and verdant like a summer field. Caught by the sun's reflection to glow and glitter with the sparkling sea, they were fringed by lashes incredibly thick . . . incredibly long. Enchanting.

Absurd things to notice when she needed rescuing, not an assessment of her attributes.

"It's all right," he assured her, quickly, huskily. "Just lie still. My boat isn't fifty yards away. Relax, and I'll get you there."

She stared at him, and the wild-eyed fear slowly faded from her features. Beautiful features. Completely classic. Slender cheeks and high bones, a full red mouth, defined and lusciously shaped, high forehead, high, nicely arched brows. Nice nose. Small, and straight. No, not straight, tilted just slightly . . .

Flynn groaned inwardly with vast impatience with himself; he gave the water a strenuous push, and surged toward the *Bella Christa.*

Juan had lowered the ladder and stood ready to help him. He reached down to lift the girl from the water. "Ahh! She weighs nothing, *amigo!* So petite . . ."

22

As Flynn climbed up the ladder, Juan was already hurrying into the cabin, calling out for Donald, Flynn's valet on land, his chef on board the *Bella Christa*.

Flynn followed Juan, heedless of the water that dripped from him to the plush carpeting of the main salon. Juan, just as heedless of the French Provincial sofa, laid the girl upon it. She whimpered slightly, and her eyelids fluttered. Then Donald, very correct in a white sailing uniform with a navy jacket, reached her side, an ammonia stick in his hand. He knelt beside her and broke the stick in his fingers beneath her nose. "Oh!" she protested, trying to escape the pungent odor. Her eyes opened fully. She glanced about herself with alarm; her eyes fell upon each of three men, and she pulled herself quickly to a sitting position.

"Where . . . am I?" she demanded with alarm.

Donald backed away. "I'll get some brandy, sir," he told Flynn. "And a robe for the lady."

"You are quite all right, Señorita," Juan supplied as Flynn took Donald's place, kneeling beside her and staring at her anxiously.

"You're aboard my yacht, the *Bella Christa*," Flynn told her. "You are perfectly all right."

"Oh . . . thank God!" she murmured. Her eyes closed, and she leaned against the couch once again. She was a mystery—a mystery that puzzled Flynn incredibly, but he couldn't help remaining silent for a minute to study the girl. She was an American; her Yankee accent had given her away immediately. Yanks never could master the Queen's English, he thought, but not without a certain amusement directed at himself, for neither his years at Oxford—nor the summer at the American naval academy—had done much to curb the brogue in his own speech.

23

An American woman . . . floating on a plank in the waters off Costa del Sol . . .

A socialite?

She was stunning. More so now, incongruous in the stylish bikini on the period furniture. She was tanned to a beautiful, glistening golden color; her hair, beginning now to dry, appeared to be a luxurious auburn, deep, yet flaming with color. A green-eyed redhead, yet no freckles sprinkled over her flesh. Her skin was entirely gold and smooth and as sleek as her long, shapely limbs. Her waist was wickedly slender, her breasts wickedly full as they mounded above the skintight, enhancing white of the bikini top.

Draped across the sofa, she was sinfully appealing. A woman couldn't have tried to appear more appealing. Tried? She had been washed up aboard a plank. Apparently the victim of an accident—or an attack? And yet, with her assets, she was able to be both disheveled and . . . totally alluring. The urge to rescue and protect . . .

And also covet. Who was she?

Donald cleared his throat as he reappeared with a snifter of brandy. Flynn lifted the girl's head; her eyes flew open once again. "Sip this," he murmured. "It's brandy."

She took a sip of the brandy, coughed and sputtered, then pushed the snifter away. "Thank you," she whispered. Her expression was lovely and vulnerable, lost and totally dazed.

"Do you know who you are?" he asked her.

Her eyes focused on him. "Of course! Oh, I am so sorry! Here I am . . . dripping all over your lovely sofa . . ."

Flynn waved away her distress. "Don't worry about the bloody sofa. Who are you, miss? What happened to you?"

Her eyes met his, lifted to Juan's, then returned to his. "My name is Brittany Martin—I'm an American, vacationing at Costa del Sol. I was terribly foolish—I mean, I'd been warned

24

about this 'El Drago' who has been attacking pleasure craft—
but I suppose I didn't really believe the stories! Anyway, I just
felt this terrible need to sail! Perhaps you understand—oh,
surely, you must! I had to feel the wind and the sea spray—
please, don't laugh!"

Flynn wasn't about to laugh. He was staring at her incredulously. "El Drago?"

"Don't tell me you haven't heard of him! It's my under-
standing that he's been the scourge of these waters—the dismay of the police!"

Flynn stood and walked past the couch, stretching as he
stared through the salon's upper sheet windows. He felt Juan's
dark eyes upon him, and the girl's.

He turned back to her.

"What happened?" he demanded tensely.

"Why, I . . . I . . . ." She floundered for a moment; her
lashes fell to shield her eyes. Then those dark, seductive fans
fluttered and raised; her chin was high, but a sheen of mois-
ture dazzled her eyes to an emerald brilliance. "I was in a ten-
foot craft, a little catamaran rented from my hotel, La Casa
Verde. I . . . I never saw the sloop come about—it rammed
me. Then there were suddenly all these . . . men in the
cabin, and I heard a man speak—"

"In English?"

"Ah, yes. With a Spanish accent."

"And then?" Flynn prompted quietly.

She lowered her head. "He had already taken my bag . . .
and he demanded to know if I had anything else. I . . . said
. . . obviously not. He terrified me. I was afraid of being
murdered or . . . murdered. He came toward me—"

"You saw him in the dark?"

"No, I heard him. And when he was near I . . . I kicked
out as wildly as I could. I hit him—I heard him grunt with the

25

pain. But I didn't wait. I tore out of the cabin and back to the deck. And then I dove over the side and—well, that's the last I remember until I opened my eyes and saw you!"

Juan began to make disgusted, tcking noises—he cursed softly in Spanish against the men who could do such a thing to such a lovely and vulnerable woman.

Flynn walked back to her and placed a hand upon her shoulder. It appeared very large and rough against the satin texture of her skin. His knuckles grazed lightly, reassuringly, over her cheek.

"You must have been very brave," he said softly. "So small a woman, tackling a man reputed to be so fierce."

She wasn't looking at him; her lashes were lowered again. His hand remained near her cheek. He felt her shiver—or was it a shudder?

"I—I wasn't particularly brave," she murmured. "Just . . . ah, desperate."

"I see."

"You are very lucky, Señorita," Juan said solemnly.

"Yes, lucky," she murmured.

Flynn smiled, lifting her chin with his forefinger. "And I still insist—courageous and resourceful."

"No . . ."

Those damn lashes! They shielded her eyes at will.

"You have nothing to worry about now," he told her softly. "You're quite safe on board the *Bella Christa*. We'll head back in, and take you to the authorities." Flynn saw Donald waiting with a soft terry robe. He raised his hand slightly and Donald stepped forward. Flynn took the robe and placed it gently around her shoulders. She gave him a smile of gratitude that was so warm and beautiful, it would have surely melted ice.

Yes, ice. And though he felt a bit like ice at that moment,

he couldn't resist the silken web of fascination that she spun with each word and movement.

"Donald will escort you to a cabin—" He paused, glancing at her left hand quickly, "—Miss Martin. I'm sure you'll wish to rest after such an ordeal."

"Thank you, so very much, Mr.—"

"Colby. Flynn Colby."

She laughed suddenly, delightedly. *"The* Flynn Colby?" She seemed truly startled—very surprised. Pleasantly, curiously so. Her inquiring smile was like warm honey.

He raised a brow, and she fanned those lashes over her cheeks once again, a slight blush staining her cheeks. "I'm sorry, but you've quite a reputation."

"Have I? For what?"

"Oh . . . for being an intriguing Englishman, of course!" She bit her lip, then shrugged as if admitting her knowledge about him to be pure gossip. "A fabulously wealthy and reckless playboy—so they say."

"I'm Scottish," he told her, but he allowed a slight grin to play about his lips; he neither denied her words, nor encouraged them, but turned to his darkly handsome friend. "Ms. Martin, allow me to introduce Señor Juan Lopez, a native of our fair Costa del Sol, and an outstanding pillar of the community. He owns most of the resorts, and is sometimes a liaison with British diplomatic officials."

Juan somehow clipped his bare feet together and very formally bowed low over her hand. "I am charmed, Señorita!"

"Oh, no, Señor. The pleasure is mine," she responded sweetly.

What a face! Flynn thought. An angel in heaven should have such a face. A mixture of innocence and sultry, beguiling beauty. A voice as low and sweet as wine . . .

"Now that we have met, Señorita," Juan told her, "I hope

that I shall see you again about Costa del Sol. Perhaps you would be so kind as to—"

"Oh, no!" Brittany Martin exclaimed suddenly, clutching the white terry robe about her with dismay filling her features.

"What, Señorita?" Juan asked with alarm.

"I . . . I don't know what I'm going to do!" she murmured ruefully. She lifted her hands and grimaced. "He has taken my money, my credit cards—everything!"

"Oh, Señorita! You mustn't worry about such petty things when you have walked away with your life and health! My dear girl! After such a violent confrontation with El Drago, we must be grateful just to have you with us!"

"Oh, I am grateful for that!" she exclaimed. But Flynn noted that her lashes fell in a low sweep over her cheeks again, and again. She shuddered—remembering her confrontation? "I just don't know what I will do."

"You can call home from my villa—" Juan began.

Flynn chuckled softly to interrupt. He crossed his arms idly over his chest, and spoke huskily. "Juan, *mi amigo!* I believe I'm the one who actually fished our mermaid from the sea— the lady must be my guest." He smiled at the girl. "Don't be alarmed by my reputation. My life-style has been outrageously exaggerated. I'm thirty-three and fairly affluent and I'm afraid that's all you need to make the newspapers these days. You've really nothing to fear. Donald and a number of servants reside at my *casa.*"

She smiled with gratitude. "Thank you both, so very much. I'm not at all afraid—just thankful. I hope that I can solve things quickly."

"I don't believe, Ms. Martin, that you could possibly outstay your welcome. Hell, I'm sure, would bloody well freeze first. And you mustn't worry—calls and resources can take time."

28

"I'm just afraid that . . ." She hesitated with a rueful grimace. "My parents are off somewhere—Germany, or Switzerland, I believe—on a second honeymoon. I'm going to have to track them down. I don't wish to get in your way or disturb your life."

"As I said," Flynn told her softly, "you are welcome—indefinitely."

"No strings attached, miss," Donald said, very suddenly and very properly, staring at his employer—then Juan—rather than Brittany, as if he were reminding both of the men that they were promising good behavior rather than assuring Brittany.

Flynn gazed at Donald, mildly curious by the man's quick, protective attitude. He was a little bemused. Women came and went—Donald was polite and courteous to them all. But this one . . . it seemed his staid employee was a little bit under a sea-spell of enchanted fantasy himself.

Flynn laughed. "Donald! That you should have to say such a thing to our guest! No strings attached, Ms. Martin."

She had colored slightly. "Mr. Colby, as I said, I'm not afraid."

But was she? he wondered. She seemed very tense. He kept smiling. "Let Donald see you to a cabin now, Ms. Martin. You must feel quite sea-logged. Enjoy a shower, and get some rest. You've been through one ordeal, the police might be another."

"The police?"

"Yes, of course. You'll want to report El Drago. Perhaps the police will be able to catch the culprit this time."

"Oh, yes!" she agreed. Then, almost in aftermath, she added a quiet, "Of course."

"It's unlikely," Juan murmured with a shake of his head. He looked at Flynn. "El Drago could be anywhere by now."

"That's the pity of it," Flynn agreed.

"I suppose I must agree with Juan," Brittany said, "and be glad that I am here now, with you. My things are small loss—thanks to your assistance."

"You've made our day, Ms. Martin. Seafarers dream of plucking beauties from the sea; we've managed to do just that."

Her eyes were downcast; she grimaced slightly. "You're very kind."

"Not at all," Flynn said. "But you are shivering. Juan and I won't detain you any longer."

She gave him a tremulous grin, then stood, wavering slightly. Juan was there to steady her instantly. She rewarded Juan with one of those beautiful, rueful smiles, then righted herself. Donald stepped forward. "Right this way, miss. I'll bring you tea in half an hour, if that will please you."

"Oh, yes, Donald, thank you very much—"

She had started to follow the valet; she stopped, and turned back. "Thank you both so very much," she murmured. "So very, very much."

And then she was gone.

The two men watched the path of departure for several seconds in silence. Then Juan turned to Flynn.

"A little mermaid," he murmured.

"Hmm. A little mermaid," Flynn agreed.

Juan cocked his head. His expression was a bit curious, a bit wary—and more than a little bit amused.

"You started the day with the fantasy, Flynn."

"Maybe I did," Flynn mused. He arched a brow to Juan. "Fantasy seems a bit thick, though, don't you think?"

"That's what happens when a myth begins," Juan warned.

"Apparently," Flynn said thoughtfully. He rubbed his chin, frowning as he stared at Juan. "Well, *amigo*, what do you think?"

"About mermaids?" Juan's dark eyes twinkled. "Frankly, I had always wondered what a normal hombre would do with one. Gaze at her beauty, touch her hair—but a fin would stand in the way of a great and fulfilling romance!"

"Ah—but this mermaid has no fin."

"True," Juan murmured. Then his tone lowered, and his dark eyes grew very serious. "So you tell me, my friend, what do you think."

"Mermaids," Flynn said slowly, "are not real. We both know that a mermaid is a creature of a seaman's fantasy—and his desire."

"Yes," Juan agreed softly. "We both know that. But what if the mermaid is unaware that . . . mermaids are not real?"

Flynn smiled grimly. "That is something I intend to find out."

Juan watched his friend's face. "Beyond a doubt, she is beautiful, Flynn. Eyes like the cat; hair of fire. A temptress, if I've ever seen one."

Flynn grinned at Juan. "Yes. But many women are beautiful. Or perhaps all are beautiful."

Juan laughed out loud. "But we both know that this one is unique."

"What are you getting at, *mi amigo?*"

Juan shrugged and picked up the brandy bottle, pouring himself a small portion, twirling it about in the glass.

"I was just thinking about Greek legend."

"Greek legend?" Flynn chuckled and decided he could do with a brandy himself. He swallowed down his two fingers full, wincing as he felt the fire in his lungs. "Let's hear this," he told Juan wryly.

"I'm sure you know Homer's story. The Greeks left Troy, but Odysseus was beset with tempests from then on. He lis-

31

tened to the song of the sirens, and could have been lost upon the rocks."

"But he was aware that there was a siren, and he had himself bound to the mast."

"Yes."

"So?"

"Perhaps I should tie you to the mast."

"And what about you, Juan?"

"All right." Juan shrugged amiably. "Perhaps we should both be bound."

"That would cause a bit of a problem."

"*Sí.*"

"Our siren is a bit of a mystery—and it's hard to solve mysteries, bound to the mast."

"I believe," Juan said slowly, watching his brandy twirl once again, "that we are, perhaps, evenly met."

"Yes, evenly met," Flynn agreed. He was no longer chuckling, or grinning. His tone had taken on a tension and solemnity. "But . . . I intend to take and use any edge that I can get."

CHAPTER TWO

Brittany stroked the tortoise-shell brush through her hair and stared blankly at her reflection in the mirror. She set the brush down on the old Spanish dresser and gazed at her hands. Belatedly, they were shaking.

She willed it to stop; the shaking only increased and she set the brush down. Feeling horribly weak-kneed, she hurried to the bed to sit, pressing her temples tightly between thumbs and forefingers.

Now she just felt ill.

It's okay, she tried to assure herself. She had carried it off. She was here; she had been accepted. As she had planned, her story had been excellent, and everything was going exactly as it should be going . . .

No, it wasn't. Not at all. She was in way over her head. So far over her head that she could barely breathe; she could barely think.

"I need a drink."

She whispered the words, heard herself, and bit her lip. She was insane. She had to be—to be here. Grief had made her mad. But could madness last that long? She had planned this trip, planned it all out with terrible bitterness and purpose as soon as the man from Scotland Yard had told her that there simply wasn't a thing in the world that could be done.

33

And isn't that why you're here? Because it isn't fair, it isn't just, and you can't accept that verdict?

Yes, of course, that was all true. But she shouldn't be here anyway, and if she hadn't found the newspaper article about El Drago when she had been cleaning the stupid bird cage, she would have never attempted such an absurd stunt.

Now, in Flynn Colby's house, she was out of her league. A feeling that had touched her as soon as she had opened her eyes, as soon as she had seen him, really seen him, face to face. Felt him, the power of his body, the economy of his movement. The cast of his eyes, the sound of his voice.

Oh, God. What if she had to face him? Face him right now, blanched and pale and trembling?

It would be all right, she promised herself desperately. It would be all right. She could shake now. She clenched and unclenched her fists. Her fingers stubbornly persisted in trembling. If she should have to face Flynn Colby soon, she could surely convince him that she was still suffering from the aftermath of her horrible confrontation with El Drago.

Think of something else besides panic! she commanded herself.

She turned around, surveying the beautiful room that had been given her, then closed her eyes to reenvision her first images of the house. Mr. Flynn Colby knew how to live in style. The *casa* was perfect for the hot sun and breezes of the Costa del Sol. Everything was white or shell peach. Long open breezeways connected around a huge courtyard and atrium on two levels; shutters could be opened to the air or closed against the heat, and within the rooms opening off of the four long corridors, everything was of the highest quality, the zenith of understated elegance. Tile, marble, golden fixtures, stained glass.

Her room was huge, open and airy. The bed was raised

upon a dais in the far center; it was massive and covered with a fur that looked like llama. With its old squared canopy, it looked like something out of a castle.

Cool Mexican tiles stretched across the floor; the dressers were heavy oak, shining with care. The walls were that shell pink that seemed so prominent here, a color that repelled heat. But they weren't bare. Even in her room—a guest room —there was nothing left to the ordinary. Two of the paintings on the wall were Picassos. The third was a Dali. She was certain that they were originals.

The bed faced twin French doors that led to the balcony. The balcony overlooked a rose garden and sparkling fountain with Neptune, king of the sea, standing guard.

Brittany sighed nervously, walked to the dais, and cast herself onto the bed, staring up at the canopy above it. She started to shake all over again, amazed that she was really here.

She had to be insane. She would never be able to carry it off, and who was she kidding to think that she could possibly trap a swindler and trick him into returning to England— especially when she didn't know who the man was?

Very especially when that man just might be Flynn Colby.

She closed her eyes tightly and inhaled a deep breath. She couldn't panic now. She had plunged in head first, and she was just going to have to see it through to the end.

There was a knock on the door. Brittany sat up quickly, nervously clutching her robe about her throat.

"Yes?"

Donald opened the door and stood there very properly and cleared his throat. There was a gray clothing bag balanced over his shoulder.

"Mr. Colby took the liberty of sending for some clothing,

Ms. Martin. He hopes you'll accept the things without worry, and that the fit will be sufficient for the time being."

"Oh," Brittany murmured, catching her breath and lowering her lashes quickly, and then her head to hide a stubborn flush. What was she doing? she asked herself with dismay. She didn't want to take anything from Flynn Colby. She felt horribly embarrassed; like a fortune hunter—or worse.

"Ms. Martin?"

"I—I'm very grateful to Mr. Colby," Brittany murmured. "Thank you, Donald. I suppose I can't keep walking around in a robe."

"Certainly not. Tomorrow you will, of course, be able to get your own things from the hotel. But for tonight . . . well, just as Mr. Colby wishes, I, too, hope that we can make you comfortable."

"Thank you, Donald. You've been more than kind."

"Not at all, miss." Donald beamed. He moved into the room with the clothing bag and hung it in the wardrobe by the bathroom door. He smiled and started to leave her, then paused. "Mr. Colby dines at eight. Will that be convenient for you, Ms. Martin?"

"Yes, perfectly, thank you."

There was no clock in the room, but Brittany had just heard a faint echo of chimes from somewhere in the house. It could only be minutes after seven.

Donald smiled again and left, closing the door behind him. Brittany felt her heart take on a thunderous pounding.

"Mr. Colby dines at eight." . . .

Mr. Colby. Flynn Colby.

She felt it again. The horrible trembling. It wasn't just in her hands, it seized hold of her limbs, fluttered like butterflies in her stomach, terrorized her heart. She really had to be insane to be here. At best, he had ten times her sophistication. At worst . . .

He was a swindler and con artist. Charming, beguiling, and very attractive. His body was muscled and toned, gold from the sun, agile . . . and uniquely fluid in movement. His eyes seemed to rivet one to them. They were blue . . . no, gray, or perhaps some shade in between. Perhaps they were blue when he laughed and they sparkled, and then smoked to a gray when his mood became more serious. Just like his smile. It was nice. Full, and wide.

But she could well imagine that smile tightening. Fading. Compressing into a grim line. Brittany shivered suddenly, wondering if Flynn Colby ever lost his perfect manners; if that air of courteous control ever left him. His face . . . it was so arresting when he smiled. But would those masculine features lose their charisma if they sallowed and tightened in anger? Or would they be equally attractive—just more dangerously so?

Brittany gave herself a little shake. She'd been reading too much about the man, and half of what she read had probably been invention anyway. Of course, she'd had to read about him. She'd read about every British national living in Costa del Sol who had been in London at the time of Alice's death. Brice had produced his list of those who had departed England and she had carefully spent two weeks investigating the men as best she could. There had been only six names on the list—three of which corresponded with those names she'd discovered in the newspaper.

Two of the men worked for a British government concern. One was a father of five, and the other barely nineteen. Brittany had, perhaps foolishly, dismissed them both.

Foolishness—or instinct? Instinct said she was right. The scam that had wiped out her aunt's finances had been a clever

37

one; played often enough, it could reap a small fortune. The guilty party had to be living very well—which was why she had also dismissed another of the names. Jim Thorpe—according to an ex-landlady Brittany had managed to question—was a "bum of an artist—selling watercolors for shillings to tourists."

Brittany's field had been narrowed to those three original names. Oh, there were any number of Britons living the golden life at Costa del Sol. But only these three had been in London at the crucial time.

Flynn Colby, Ian Drury, and Joshua Jones.

She had convinced herself she was not afraid of any of them. She could handle herself well—as long as no one gave her more than two forks at the dinner table. She kept telling herself she wasn't afraid, and she was no more worried now than she had been when she had plunged into the water. She could swim—she could take care of herself. Even against the Flynn Colbys of the world.

Flynn Colby. One of the world's ten most eligible bachelors, according to several popular magazines. It seemed that he was a favorite of gossip columns in a multitude of countries, despite the fact that he avoided the press. Oh well, Brittany mused, people loved an enigma. Yet there was really very little tangible information about him to be had. No one had really managed to quite pin down just what it was he did to keep an inherited fortune afloat. He'd been married once in his early twenties—a very proper match with an earl's daughter—but the marriage had ended in divorce in less than a year. Since then, he had raced his yachts around the world; he played polo, but really: was that enough to keep living in this kind of style?

He couldn't be her man, Brittany thought passionately. He was so—magnetic.

But then a magnetic man was just the one to create such a scam.

He just didn't seem right, Brittany thought with a sigh. Not with those sharp, direct eyes. Not with the way he could look . . . at a woman.

Or maybe he was all the better a suspect because of those eyes and his subtly overwhelming masculinity. Maybe she just didn't want him to be the culprit because of that palpable tension she felt each time he was near.

Don't be a fool! she warned herself sternly.

Impulsively Brittany stood and hurried to the clothing bag Donald had hung in the wardrobe. A flood of color seemed to cascade into her hands as she unzipped it. Froth and silk—the bag contained a cool cocktail gown of emerald silk and a peignoir set in peach, lightly furred about the neck and hemline.

For a moment Brittany was enchanted by the sheer softness of the materials. Then she allowed them to fall from her hands in a moment of doubt and self-loathing.

What was the value of such clothing? And did it really matter? Colby probably didn't care. She wondered what he thought of her. Had he believed her story? Or did that even matter to him? A slow flush suffused Brittany's cheeks again. Flynn Colby was the type of man who attracted women. Like a football hero or rock star, he simply attracted women, and maybe two particular types of women: those who wanted just to touch such a man and enjoy what they could, and . . . those who simply wanted to be bought.

He was probably assuming she fell into the second category.

And in a way, she told herself dismally, it was true. She hadn't the funds to stay on at Costa del Sol; and if she wanted justice, she had to stay.

Brice had told her point blank that there wasn't a thing in the world that the British police could do. Not unless the man returned to British soil—or appeared in a country that did have an extradition agreement with the British.

But what was she doing? Brice didn't even know what she was up to. If he did, he'd tell her she was a fool. That she was in deep water way over her head . . .

"What is the matter with me?" she whispered irritably. She had known ever since she decided to cast herself into the sea that she planned to use this man—whether he was guilty or innocent. And she had rationalized at that time that she certainly couldn't hurt the man if he was innocent—entertaining a guest for a couple of weeks would be no hardship for him.

"So why the cold feet now?" she quizzed again out loud.

Planning to use him was a lot different from actually being here. Feeling like . . . feeling awful.

She had never worried about his reputation with women. Not in her planning stage. She had fought very competitively in a field where men were known to have the edge of strength and she had always held her own. And in her chosen profession, she'd come across all types—the golden and muscled; the suave and the cool beach boy toughs. She'd also learned to handle the worst of them; once she had learned to break the hold of a drowning swimmer, she could master any overambitious date.

She knew that when she needed to be, she could be hard and assertive. She felt she was capable of seeing her goal and heading straight for it. She was impatient with the idea of backing down, and leaving things to fate. To Brittany, it was impossible to forget what had happened. She had made her plans—fully aware that they could be dangerous as well as uncomfortable. She had to move forward—and keep in mind that Flynn Colby was just a man. Perhaps he did intend to seduce her. Fine. She needed him, and she needed his connections. She had to allow herself to be charmingly seduced—to a point. Unless he was the guilty party, of course. Then she would hope that he rotted in a jail cell until he was far too old to be much of a lady-killer. And if he wasn't guilty . . . Maybe he would even understand.

Flynn Colby was different from any other man she had known.

She could feel him when he wasn't even really near her. He moved with extra energy; his eyes were more intense than the average man's. His voice could be a caress . . . or a whiplash. She barely knew him, yet when he looked at her, she felt he knew her through and through. There was just that manner about him. Courteous charm, complete confidence. It was easy to see why he had become such an international fascination. He was different—as rugged and sharp as an uncut diamond.

"Maybe it's because he's a crook!" she chided herself impatiently. She had to forget feelings. Turn her back on any situation which made her uneasy.

If she didn't, someone was going to get away with what amounted to murder.

In short, she had to accept Flynn Colby's charity, and she had to continue to play the role of a lost and sheltered socialite—being careful that she also kept her wits about her at all times. It was her only chance.

Grinding her teeth together hard, Brittany plucked the clothing from the floor. She tossed the peignoir set on the bed, and headed into the bathroom with the cocktail gown. Carefully folded into the elegant green depths was a set of equally elegant lingerie. Handmade lace panties, a teddy and stockings. Perfect for her size and the outfit. Perfect—and alarmingly intimate.

She bathed quickly and dressed, only realizing then that

41

she hadn't any shoes—nor did she have the slightest idea of where she was supposed to go for dinner. From Flynn's yacht, they had gone directly to the police station—a horrendous experience as she had tried to remember her lie word for word —and when they had reached the *casa*, she had only seen the corridors briefly, downstairs, and then up.

She sat nervously on the bed again, running her fingers over the llama fur. Donald would probably come back for her.

Too nervous to sit on the bed for long, Brittany returned to the dresser and picked up the tortoise-shell brush again. She was startled by her own reflection. The emerald of the dress brought a flame to her eyes; they were wide and their color seemed to dance and shimmer along with that of the silk. Her hair fell over it in tumbling waves that gleamed a rich and radiant chestnut; she had never seen herself look better.

Someone really was a connoisseur—of clothing and women.

"*Touché*, Mr. Colby," she murmured to the mirror. "We're both after something. We'll just have to see who succeeds."

As if in answer, there was a single, sharp rap on her door. "Ms. Martin? It's Flynn."

Brittany stared at her reflection a moment longer. Again, that annoying flush of color stained her cheeks. Her heart thundered. She couldn't panic . . .

"Ms. Martin? Are you ready?"

She forced herself to smile; the color faded. Brittany spun gracefully in the silk and threw open the door.

"Mr. Colby, I'm so sorry to keep you waiting!"

He was dressed for dinner. So often things were casual at Costa del Sol. Not Flynn Colby, not this evening. His dinner jacket was white; his trousers and vest were mahogany brown. He was clean shaven and his scent was not that of aftershave, but rather of clean male flesh, and it was somehow all the more alluring. He smiled, and the whiteness of his teeth contrasted sharply with the depth of his tan and Brittany was reminded again that this was a man known for his natural allure. It was a nice smile: friendly, open. His manner was not alarming or threatening. His appeal alone was both.

"You look absolutely wonderful," he told her.

"Thank you," Brittany said. She smiled. "And thanks to you. I can't tell you how much I appreciate the loan of the gown—"

"It's not a loan. It's a gift. A 'welcome to my *casa*.'"

She allowed herself to smile. "I can't accept it as a gift, Mr. Colby. I would love to accept it as a loan."

He shrugged. "As you wish. A loan then."

"An elegant loan," Brittany murmured.

"Ah, but what man who fishes a mermaid from the sea could offer anything less than the elegance she deserves?"

Brittany laughed, tilting her chin upward in challenge. She had to; without her shoes, she stood at five four. He was almost a foot taller than that. "Mr. Colby," she told him lightly—but with calm certainty, "you're very smooth."

He laughed in return. "Flynn—please. And not really. I merely call it as I see it. I did fish you from the sea, and by circumstance, you're my guest. There is a bit of fantasy to it. Please don't begrudge my whim of the dress—it is perfect. Shall we go to dinner?"

Brittany grimaced and looked down at her feet. "I'd love to go to dinner—if you don't mind stockinged feet."

His smile fell. "Shoes! I remembered everything except shoes."

Yes, he had remembered everything. Definitely in the intimate apparel line. And it seemed that he had made the selections himself. Brittany kept her smile intact. "Please, don't worry. I appreciate the fact that you've been able to help me at all. From the way my day began . . ."

She gave a very convincing little shudder. It wasn't difficult. Maybe because he was near.

"Ah, yes, your brush with El Drago," Flynn said somberly. "I suppose we both must be thankful that you're here at all . . ." He set a comforting arm about her shoulders. "I'll have to do my best to set that awful incident from your mind. Come on—I'll fix us drinks. I'm sure Donald can scrape up something in the shoe department, and then we'll have dinner and hopefully I'll convince you that it was all just a nightmare . . . nothing more than a fabrication of the mind."

Brittany gazed up at him uneasily as he escorted her along the eastern corridor. He was staring straight ahead, no longer smiling, but giving no indication that his words were anything other than sincere. He must have sensed her eyes on him; he gazed down to her, and once again smiled. There was only moonlight and an occasional torch in the corridor; she saw a strange cast to his eyes, a sparkle. His features seemed more gaunt; sharper. And his smile seemed just a little bit . . .

"What size?"

"Pardon me?"

"Your shoes—they must be very small. Five, six?"

"Ah, yes, a size five and a half. But Mr. Colby—"

"Flynn. You are a guest, and I tend to think of my guests as my friends."

"Flynn," Brittany murmured, "please, you're doing so much already. Don't worry about shoes; it's quite warm—"

"I wouldn't dream of having you run around barefoot. It's absolutely no problem. I apologize sincerely for such a lack of thought on my behalf."

Brittany started to protest again, but Flynn had paused before a wrought-iron door which proved to be an elevator cage. He escorted Brittany in, and as the cage began to lower, muted light rose around them.

"We're dining on the terrace," he told her briefly in explanation.

The elevator came to a halt. Flynn pushed open the cage door, and once again, escorted Brittany before him.

The table was set on the patio, surrounded by flowers, foliage, and bubbling fountains. It was a small table, round, covered with a snowy white cloth and set with shimmering silver and crystal. Nearby, fitting in a curve around the rear corridor wall, was a bar. Flynn left her staring at the table and the fountains and flowers to slip behind it.

"What can I get you?"

"Rum and Coke, light please."

He arched a brow, lifting a bottle to comply with her wishes. "Not the last of the big-time drinkers, I see."

"No."

Brittany gazed at him as he replaced the rum bottle, squirted Coke into her glass, and fixed himself something amber on the rocks. He smiled at her, then she realized that he was gazing over her shoulder. Donald was there. She hadn't heard his arrival.

"Donald," Flynn said pleasantly, "I seem to have made a major mistake in Ms. Martin's wardrobe for the evening—I forgot all about shoes. Think we could find a pair somewhere, size 5 1/2."

"Certainly," Donald said. He bowed slightly to Brittany, then addressed his next comment to Flynn. "Maria says that dinner can be served whenever you like."

"Fine, Donald, fine. If you'll see about some shoes for our Ms. Martin here, I'll escort her around the atrium. Then I think we'll be ready."

Donald left them. Flynn came around from behind the bar, handing Brittany her drink, then taking her elbow to guide her along.

"Well, Brittany, what do you think of my home?" he asked her.

It was an innocent enough question; she wondered why she felt as if his eyes were boring into her soul.

She met them with a smile in her own. "It's lovely," she answered honestly enough, pausing then to study the intricate little vein lines on what appeared to be a huge philodendron. The atrium was exquisite—almost like a well-planned rain forest. She dropped the leaf, then returned her attention to him with polite interest. "But I'm curious, though—what brings an Englishman to live in the south of Spain?"

"Scotsman," he corrected her again with a slight grin. "There is a difference."

"Yes, I'm sorry. I've spent enough time in London to know that," Brittany murmured apologetically. "But the question— if it isn't too rude—still stands."

He cocked his head with a grimace and a shrug. "I don't live here full time. I keep a home here because I like the sun —and the water. The warmth. It's a beautiful place."

"Yes, it is," Brittany mused. She was looking up at him again, and they were very close. She turned and followed a narrow tile path that led through a maze in the heart of the atrium.

"Where else do you live?" she asked idly, pausing again to survey a miraculously large and lovely rose.

"Scotland," he answered, following behind her. "The old family castle, you know. And London—I keep a flat."

"Nothing in the States?" she inquired, running a finger like a breath over a petal of the orchid.

He was standing beside her again. She could feel the brush of his jacket against her arm as he moved to the plant, snapping the orchid from its stem. Then he looked at her again, his eyes following the path of his hand as he slipped the orchid behind her ear. She felt as if she could barely breathe; tremors quaked inside of her and where he touched her, she burned.

"I've been thinking about letting a flat in New York," he said, adjusting the flower.

"Apartment," Brittany murmured.

"Pardon?"

"Ah . . . apartment. In New York, you would call it an apartment."

"Oh, yes."

Brittany took a step backward, annoyed that the gift of an orchid could make her stutter. She touched the flower herself and smiled. "Thank you—it's a lovely flower."

A small smile played about his lips. "Where do you live, Brittany? Are you familiar with New York? Perhaps you could suggest a suitable . . . apartment complex."

"I'm afraid I don't know much about New York," Brittany murmured quickly, continuing down the path. She sure as hell didn't know what to tell a man who owned a castle! She was getting too nervous, she warned herself, but she kept talking anyway. "I live in Florida. West Palm Beach. They've a marvelous polo club, and Daddy's just wild about the game."

She moved quickly along the path, barely seeing an array of bougainvillea and another of the delightful, bubbling fountains. Dismay had filled her. What on earth had prompted her to say such a thing? She knew less about polo than she did about the fashionable haunts of New Yorkers. And wasn't polo one of his hobbies—second only to his racing enthusiasm? Great. Just great! she charged herself.

"I've been there," Flynn said from behind her, and she felt her heart take a giant downward plunge. "It is a good field."

Brittany spun around, smiling broadly. "I'm glad you found

47

it so. To be honest, I rarely go." She wrinkled up her nose. "Horrible, isn't it—but I'm afraid of horses."

"You don't ride?"

"No."

"A pity," he said idly. "I've a full stable out back. A wonderful way to see the area."

"Perhaps I can learn."

"Perhaps. I'd love to teach you."

He was next to her again. For some reason, she never saw him move, yet he was always there. Those steel-blue eyes were always on her. That polite, slightly amused curl always seemed to play about his lips—and then it would be gone, as if she had imagined it. He wasn't touching her, and then he was—taking her arm like the perfect escort, only he wasn't just an idle escort; not when she felt his touch as if he were energy and fire . . .

"I believe we've given Donald time enough to find some shoes. Shall we head back to the patio and the table? I must admit, I'm starving."

"Of course," Brittany murmured.

He didn't glance her way as they followed the tile path back to the table; she found herself fighting to study his profile.

"There's Donald." At last he gazed at her, grinning. "Seems you'll no longer have to patter around barefoot."

"I hope these will do, Ms. Martin," Donald offered. He held a pair of gold strap sandals that gave the appearance of being brand new. Brittany accepted the shoes, thanked Donald, then dropped them to the floor to slip her feet inside. Perfect.

"Well, now that you're properly shod . . ." Flynn murmured. She felt his hand, lightly, at the base of her spine, directing her toward the table. She looked around for Donald as Flynn pulled out her chair, but he had silently disappeared.

"You do drink wine with dinner, Brittany?"

She murmured an assent, which probably wasn't necessary since he was already reaching into a wine bucket. He casually —almost imperceptibly—sniffed the aroma as he removed the cork, then glanced her way with his strange brand of small smile before lifting the glasses to pour.

"It's a German Riesling—1972. From the Hausfen vineyards. I hope you like it. I think that seventy-two was an excellent year."

"I'm sure it will be fine," Brittany murmured sweetly, sipping her wine.

It was awful. Dry enough to create a desert. This was supposed to be a good wine?

She smiled. "Lovely," she told him.

"Umm." He took his place across from her. Watching her. He lifted a hand; seconds later Donald was appearing with the appetizer, a plate artfully arranged with shrimp and chunks of exotic fruit upon a bed of lettuce. Brittany managed to chatter about the fruit for a while—a safe topic, she thought, as safe as her enthusiasm over the size of the delicious shrimp. But by the time they had traveled through a spinach salad, and started into the main course, a fantastic bouillabaise, Brittany found that he was querying her again. She decided she'd better stick as close to the truth as possible.

"I spend most of my time on the beach," she told him— hiding a wince each time she took a sip of the wine and trying to smile through the unpalatable taste. "The water is my life and my hobby, I suppose."

He politely arched a brow, but his eyes fell to his fingers as they played idly about the base of his wineglass. "That's it— the beach?"

She smiled—and drank more wine. "Well, of course, that's not it. There's the community, you know. And father's social calendar."

"You never had the urge to strike off into the world?"

"Not really. We've always traveled, you see."

"Yes, of course," he murmured easily. His eyes lifted; Donald was there to clear away the plates. Everything in the house seemed to work on well-oiled gears that took no more than a glance to set in motion.

"You never married?" Flynn asked, lighting a cigarette as coffee was set before them. He offered the pack to Brittany; she shook her head, wishing she did smoke just then so that she would have something to do with her hands.

"Ah, no."

"Not for lack of proposals, I assume?" he queried politely.

"For lack of the . . . right man, I suppose," Brittany murmured.

He leaned closer to her suddenly, running the tip of his thumb over her index finger. "Will he have to be rich, do you think?"

Brittany was suddenly grateful for the god-awful wine. It was, at least, allowing her to laugh like a debutante. "I haven't the faintest idea at the moment. When he comes along, I'll tell you. But really, my life is dreadfully boring. Do you really own a castle?"

"Yes."

"It must be fascinating."

"It's an endless pit that hungers for constant renovation. A financial liability that can eat you alive."

"Oh?" Brittany sipped her coffee. Money. Yes—a castle would need lots and lots of money. "Where is it?"

"The uplands. It's on a spit of land near John o'Groats—northern Scotland."

She sensed something then; in that softly pleasant burr to his voice. For all that it might be a liability, he loved that castle.

50

"Sounds lovely, though," she murmured.

"It is. Very different from here, though. The weather can be very cold and harsh, and it's a lonely place. The township is small; you see far more sheep than people there. But speaking of people, I haven't given you a chance to try and contact yours."

"Oh!" Brittany's dismay was real. Who in the hell could she try to call? She was going to have to do something . . .

He was already solving that problem for her. "It would probably be impossible to try and reach your parents, but perhaps there is a neighbor they might contact? If you just call and report your situation to somewhere near, we can sit back and relax and let time take care of your problems."

"What a wonderful idea. May I try to contact the States?"

Flynn lifted his hand again. Donald—good old Donald—was at his side immediately. "Could you bring the extension, please?"

"Right away, sir."

Extension. Great. She was going to have to call right at the table with him sitting barely an arm's distance away.

Somehow, she kept smiling.

Donald returned with the phone. Flynn picked up the receiver. "I'll get the operator for you," he told her. "In fact, if you'll just give me the number . . . ? My Spanish is probably a little better than yours."

Brittany gritted her teeth and rattled off a number. Flynn spoke in quick and fluent Spanish to the operator, then hung up. "She says it will only be a minute, but of course, in Spain . . ." He shrugged, then leaned across the table again.

"I hope you won't mind being involved in a few social events while you're here, Brittany."

"Social events?" She offered him a smile and her casual

interest; her heart seemed to be pounding double-time. "I won't mind at all, Flynn."

His lids lowered briefly over the crystal gaze of his eyes, then that compelling stare fell her way again. "I like my name the way you say it," he told her softly, the tone almost a caress. She shivered, but the moment was brief; it might have never been. He sat back. "There's a fairly large British colony here, I'm sure you're aware. An acquaintance of mine, Ian Drury, is planning a dinner party tomorrow evening. Perhaps you would attend with me."

Another hammer blow seemed to seize her heart. "I'd just love to go with you, Flynn."

"Good. I—"

The shrill ringing of the phone interrupted whatever it was that he was about to say. Brittany jumped, then stared at the phone a full second before grabbing it—a bit too hastily. An irritated voice was calling out a rapid succession of hellos.

"Hello, Monica, it's Brittany."

"Brittany! Where are you? I thought you were in London. The operator said something about Spain. I'm so sorry about your aunt, Brit. But what are you doing? When are you coming back to work—"

"Monica, please, listen to me for a minute. I've had the most frightful experience. I came for the sun, you know, and the season. But there's this nasty pirate running around here, a sea-mugger, I guess is what he is. Anyway, I'm fine; I'm at the home of Flynn Colby—he's been kind enough to take me in—"

"Flynn Colby!"

"Yes, Monica." Brittany prayed that Colby hadn't heard her friend's shriek. "Monica, I've no way to reach Mom and Dad—"

"What is this, Brittany?" Monica demanded more soberly.

"I should hope you *can't* reach them. I don't mean to be cruel, but they have been dead for ten years."

"Monica, if they should contact you," Brittany grated with sweet force, "please have them get in touch with me. I haven't a dime left, that horrible man stole everything."

"Brittany, I think you've lost your mind. You didn't have a dime to begin with."

"Just the point, Monica."

"Brittany—"

"Monica, please!" Brittany stared across the table at Flynn. Those blue-gray eyes were irrevocably on her. She plastered another smile to her lips.

"Monica, this is the world's worst connection! I'm going to have to get back to you."

"You'd better get back to me, Brittany Martin," Monica threatened. "Flynn Colby! I gather that someone is listening, but I don't like it one bit. Not one bit! You call me as soon as you can—collect. Understand?"

"Yes, yes. Thank you so much, Monica!"

Brittany replaced the receiver and tried to hide her hesitation as she looked at Flynn. He was smiling at her as he did so often; that subtle curl of amusement just barely visible.

"Is everything all right?" he asked.

"Ah, yes. Fine. Just fine. Monica hasn't heard from them yet, but as soon as she does, she'll explain the situation, and they'll be in touch."

"Wonderful," Flynn murmured.

Yes, wonderful. Brittany felt as if it had been the longest day of her life. She just wasn't sure if she could keep smiling anymore.

She pushed back her chair and stood. Flynn instantly did likewise.

"No, please, sit, Flynn. But if you'll forgive me, I'm just exhausted. Would you mind terribly if I turned in?"

"My apologies. I should have realized that you must be frightfully tired. It was such a harrowing day."

"Harrowing . . ."

"Your experience with El Drago."

"Oh, yes . . . you do understand . . ."

How was she managing to face him? Easy, she reminded herself. Because he just might be the most cunning liar of all.

"I'll walk you to your room."

"But you needn't—"

"Brittany, I wouldn't dream of not escorting you . . ."

That voice with its deep, smooth and velvet tones. The burr that caressed and hypnotized.

He could probably sell refrigerators to Eskimos.

Brittany decided to give in.

"Well, then, thank you. As always, you're incredibly kind."

Flynn smiled and took her arm. He didn't chatter; he did speak idly as they transversed the corridors, telling her about the terra-cotta sculptures in the breezeways, and how they commemorated the various gods who were important to the Spanish seafarers.

Finally they reached her door. Brittany found herself with her back to it, caught between him and the paneling.

Her breath seemed to escape her, and she could not reclaim it. The light was muted; dim, that of a candle's glow. She saw only the glitter of his eyes, blue now; the flash of white teeth in that handsome, golden face. She sensed him, the clean scent, fresh like the sea, male like the heated energy, the passion and tension that were his.

And she forgot—cleanly forgot—why she was there. That everything was a lie; that she was a lie. That she had come to trick and deceive a grand deceiver.

For a moment she was aware only that she longed to touch him and feel his touch. There would be a unique beauty in the strength of his arms about her, in the pounding of his heart. His whisper alone could touch chords of rich excitement . . .

"Good night, Flynn," Brittany said. She realized that her hands were braced against the door, that her nails were digging into the wood.

He lifted a hand slowly. He brushed her cheek with his knuckles, and his smile now did not hold its unnerving humor; it seemed . . . wistful.

She thought, perhaps, that he would linger forever. Until she gave up her grip on the door, cried out, and fell into his arms.

His hand slowly dropped.

"Good night, Brittany," he told her. And then he turned. She closed her eyes, but she could hear his footsteps as he moved down the corridor. It was a light tread. Smooth and quick, but surprisingly light.

It warned her that he could move very silently.

And that she could just find herself pounced upon when she least expected it.

CHAPTER THREE

Juan was standing in the patio when Flynn returned via the elevator. Flynn noted that his friend—who had a flair for subtly dramatic dress—was looking exceptionally sharp. His light leisure-wear suit was off-white, and in contrast, his open-neck shirt was a black silk.

Flynn quirked a brow as he approached his friend. Juan tilted his head and gave him an inquiring grin. The Spaniard was slightly the shorter of the two, and his build was slim. Flynn knew that there was a wiry strength to that slimness.

"Going out on the town tonight?" he asked Juan dryly, lifting a hand to indicate the table.

"I might ask the same of you," Juan replied.

"I doubt you dressed up for me."

"Nor, *amigo,* did you do so for me."

Flynn grimaced and sank into the chair he had recently vacated. "I've a guest in the house. Of course I dressed. And I wouldn't think of deserting her. What if she were to wake in the middle of the night, plagued by nightmares?"

Juan chuckled. He moved to the table, found a stemmed glass chilling in the ice bucket, and helped himself to the wine. Flynn watched in polite silence as Juan swallowed a sip of the wine, choked, coughed—then stared at him in amazement as he was coming up with a soft variety of curses in his native tongue.

"*Mi madre!* But what is that stuff?"

Flynn lifted his hands, grinning. "I'm not really sure. The cheapest stuff Donald could find at the market. Mixed with a little vinegar."

"You are loco, Scotsman!" Juan charged, sliding into the chair opposite Flynn. "You serve this . . . this—" Juan finally found a suitable description for horse manure in Spanish and spat it out, then continued, "to a guest? To a young lady?"

Flynn shrugged, idly drumming a drum against the table. "I told her it was a vintage German Riesling. She believed me."

"No! Anyone would know—"

"Anyone who knew wine."

"So—she does not know wine. What does that prove?"

"That she isn't any bloody socialite."

Juan shrugged. "Her manners are impeccable. Her voice . . . the lines of her face. She has elegance and breeding—"

"We're not talking about a racehorse, Juan. We're talking about a woman."

"*Sí*—but you can prove nothing against her for not spitting out your excuse for wine. Rather, it but enhances her perfection. She was too polite to insult her host."

Flynn leaned back and lit a cigarette, staring at Juan with narrowed eyes that sparkled with both amusement and reproach.

"You're bewitched, Juan. It isn't like you."

"No—I'll correct that," Juan retorted, wagging a finger at Flynn. "It is exactly like me. Me—I am hot-blooded. I love to fall in love. But you . . . you fall in love only when it fits

57

your convenience. And never with reckless passion. Yet I would say that you are—in the very least—intrigued."

"I have to be intrigued. And careful."

"Careful-bah! So she is not a socialite! She is a poor beauty, thrilled to have fallen into the good graces of Flynn Colby. Have you nothing to offer me to drink to cleanse my palate of that—"

"I know what you think of the wine." Flynn crushed out his cigarette and stood, then strode for the bar. "Brandy?"

"Fine."

Flynn proceeded to pour out the drink.

Juan watched him reflectively for a minute. "Her name is real," he said at last.

Flynn gazed up. "You've checked?"

"Yes. The police have already checked with the consulate about a new passport. She is Brittany Marie Martin, twenty-five, of Cocoa Beach, Florida, U.S.A."

Flynn walked back around the bar and set a snifter before Juan. "So her name is real." He took his seat again.

Juan waved a hand in the air impatiently. "Perhaps she is just lovestruck—entranced with a notorious figure from the pages of a magazine."

"I don't think she's terribly entranced with me."

"Ah, but she's in your *casa*. Would it were mine!"

"Seriously, Juan, I'm worried. She could be my downfall."

"You're worried? I don't believe it. How could she know anything?"

"I don't know." He lit another cigarette, exhaled, and stared musingly at the smoke as it drifted into the air. Then his gaze fell to meet Juan's directly.

"I've got a phone number for you to get on tomorrow." He called out a string of numbers. Juan briskly drew a pad and pen from his jacket to write them down. "It's Cocoa Beach—find out what you can."

"First thing," Juan agreed. "And you—what will you be doing? Entertaining your guest?"

"You know I can't. I've work to do. Funds to transfer. But tomorrow night, I'll be bringing her to Drury's dinner party."

"Will that be wise?"

Flynn shrugged. His lids lowered to give his eyes a lazy cast and he relaxed more comfortably into the chair. But even in those thin slits, there was a sharp glitter, and Juan doubted that his friend ever missed a thing—not even in sleep perhaps.

"I want to see her in action."

"Do you, I wonder?" Juan queried lightly. "Drury is a man of charisma and I think he'll find your guest charming and innocent—even if you don't."

Flynn started; his eyes opened fully. It was surprising how much Juan's suggestion jarred him. "I'll have to see that he doesn't charm her away. I don't want her getting too close to Drury. Not when I don't know what either is up to—and I have to make bloody damn sure that they don't key in on me."

Juan stood up and drained his brandy. "There are other reasons to see that another man does not take such a woman away."

"Yes, there are," Flynn agreed pleasantly.

Juan shrugged and started to walk from the table. He paused, turning back. "You know, you could just ask her exactly who she is—and what she is doing. You could, in fact, be angry. And passionately demanding."

Flynn chuckled. "No, *amigo*, I think that my way is better. I will discover things in my own way." His eyes were sharp; blue ice. "My day for demands will come—at my time, and my convenience. Until then, well, I will act out the role that she sees for me."

Juan shrugged. "As you wish. You are the boss, *amigo.*"

"*Buenas noches, Juan.· Mañana.*"

"*Mañana.* I'll give you whatever I've gotten on our mermaid at the party."

"*Bueno.*"

Juan continued on out. Flynn picked up the bottle of horrible wine, swirled it around, smiled curiously, then slowly frowned.

"Ms. Martin," he murmured aloud, "you are definitely a lovely mystery. But just what are you up to? It will be fascinating to find out. Juan has an eye for beauty, and he is right about yours. But . . ." He slipped into his chair again, sighing a little wearily.

"But I can't let you get in my way, Brittany. I just can't let you get in my way."

The upstairs corridors of the sprawling house were open beneath rounded archways to lead to huge, sun-drenched balconies. The rear of the house looked out over the ocean, and it was here, beneath a candy-striped umbrella, that Brittany sat musing the next afternoon. The view was glorious. Beneath her was the pool, and beyond that a stretch of snow beach, and to the left of the beach, where the water darkened with depth, was a private dock. Brittany could see the mast of Flynn's *Bella Christa,* listing proudly as she rocked with the small, rippling waves that touched her at her berth. There were a number of boats there too—smaller craft. Two catamarans, and several sleek speedboats.

Brittany sat back in her deck chair, enjoying the sun on her legs, and sipping the piña colada Donald had insisted she needed. It was definitely what they called The Life, but though it was fun in a way, it was disturbing in another. She was so accustomed to being busy that she was already feeling restless.

She tapped a fingernail against her glass, and sternly reminded herself that patience was a virtue. She hadn't expected Flynn Colby to be gone when she had awakened. "On business," Donald had told her. She had thought she might spend the day in his company, and come closer to an analysis of the man.

Maybe it was a good thing she'd had the day to herself, she admitted wryly. Flynn Colby might have come closer to an analysis of her. He had a talent for shifting from a question and becoming the inquisitor himself.

And then maybe he wasn't being an inquisitor at all. If you found a woman floating around on a plank and brought her home, it was certainly natural to ask questions. If a man and woman met over coffee, they naturally asked questions of one another.

The sun was starting to fall, Brittany noticed, and the sky was taking on a lovely crimson. The sea was becoming a deeper blue, and where it met the horizon, the colors created a glorious crash. Just like a little piece of paradise.

It could be paradise here—if she weren't so terribly hurt and angry. But then again, if she hadn't been such a caldron of emotion, she would never have come here in the first place. And she wouldn't have dreamt of attempting to throw herself in the path of Flynn Colby.

A chill breeze swept by with the sinking of the sun and Brittany shivered. She was glad Flynn hadn't been with her that morning when Donald had taken her to the hotel to collect her things. She had been careful about the wardrobe she had brought, but something made her think that Flynn Colby might just have looked around her room and decided that they

61

weren't the belongings of a member of the filthy rich. Donald, bless him, was too proper to oppose her in any way. She'd asked him to wait in the lobby, and he had done so with no protest. Flynn would have probably insisted on helping her.

My God, but Flynn was something! she mused. So attractive, and yet his draw wasn't on any rational level. It wasn't that he made a woman feel weak or foolishly feminine, but rather that there was something jarring and exciting and tense about him. He could touch the senses without the mind even being aware . . .

Don't make it be him, she prayed silently. Then she sighed, because she had no way of knowing yet, and if he was her crook, she knew that she would be able to hate him with total intensity.

If he was her crook. Tonight she just might be able to find out. How perfect. She had no right to feel restless; she needed to meet Ian Drury, and tonight was her perfect opportunity. Her two chief suspects in one room. Things were moving quickly and far better than she had a right to expect after plunging in so recklessly.

"Good evening."

Brittany started and turned toward the archway. Flynn was there; from his casual stance, leaned against the shell-colored wall, it seemed apparent that he had been watching her for some time.

"Hi," she returned, almost faltering. She quickly smiled and lifted her glass to the horizon. "You've truly a magnificent view here. I've been admiring it all afternoon."

He moved toward her, taking the chair opposite her. Today he was in a white knit shirt and tan slacks. She noted the ribboned muscles in his arms, and the sun-darkened breadth of his hands as he folded them casually between his knees, angling near her.

"I'm glad you like it. But then, you do seem to be a creature of the sun and sea."

"Yes, I like the water," Brittany agreed, staring out at the horizon again.

"Mermaids should."

Brittany laughed. "And you've decided I'm a mermaid?"

"What else does a man fish from the sea?"

"Nothing so fantastical, I assure you," Brittany told him. She was starting to flush again. His gaze had that effect.

"I wonder," he murmured softly, but he was grinning, and his eyes were light. There was no threat in the words. "Donald said you transferred your things over with no snags."

"Yes, we finished quite early. I want to thank you again for your hospitality. I don't know what I would have done. Even my ticket home was lost to—"

"El Drago," Flynn finished for her indignantly.

"Yes."

"Ah, well, best to forget it all. My hospitality is nothing. You're beautiful to come home to."

"Thank you." She lowered her lashes, then raised them. "Was it a hard day at the office?"

"A hard day? No, not especially." Flynn laughed. "And not at the office. I just had some time-consuming errands."

"Oh," Brittany murmured. "What do you . . . uh . . . usually do?"

He shrugged. "I haven't any usuallys. Ah, you're referring to a living?"

"I didn't mean to be rude. It's just that last night you were telling me that it is ghastly exorbitant to keep your castle going—"

"Yes, I did say that, didn't I?"

"And you seem to travel so frequently. Donald said that I was lucky the other day—that you had just returned."

"Yes—well, I follow the racing circuit, you know. There was a big cup race off Normandy last week."

And I'm supposed to assume you were in Normandy, Brittany thought. Liar! I know damned well that you were in London.

"And did you win?"

"No." Flynn stood, offering her his hand. She stared at it—it was both attractive and powerful. He wore no rings, but she imagined that the simple gold watch on his wrist was the real thing. And for some reason, something about it emphasized his healthy coloring, and the wired strength of his frame.

Snake! she thought.

"Let's take a walk on the beach," he suggested. "I think we just have time before getting ready for Drury's party."

Brittany accepted his hand. She couldn't hang him yet. She didn't have sufficient evidence.

Flynn led the way down a spiral staircase to the pool, then through the gardens to a beach path, his fingers laced through hers. Brittany followed him, hoping that her breathless laughter was flirtatious—and convincing. It was difficult when she was longing to strangle him—and confront him with the fact that he was a liar.

They reached the open beach and he drew her before him, holding her shoulders from behind as he pointed out the swimming area, and the dock beyond. She felt his breath, warm and caressing against her ear, as he spoke to her.

"While you're here, you must make this place your home, you know. Everything is at your disposal. The pool, the beach . . . the boats."

"Thank you," Brittany murmured. She clenched her jaw together to remain still with the heat of his body touching hers. She forced herself to move away leisurely. "I would certainly ask you before taking any of your things," she murmured. The sand was damp beneath her feet. The salt air was especially sweet here. She kept her eyes on the light, rippling waves.

"I'm not always around to be asked," he told her, and she sensed that he was coming near her again. "You must use what you like, when you choose."

He was standing before her. Eyes a reflection of the surf and sun, brilliant as they stared into hers.

"Do you have to be gone . . . so very much?" she heard herself whisper. It was well done. Very real—too real.

"Sometimes."

"Perhaps I could accompany you on some occasions."

"Business can be boring."

"You don't like to be bothered with business questions, do you?" Her smile was perfectly wistful; her heart was pounding away.

"That depends." His hands caught both of hers; for a moment they were joined between them. Then his were no longer holding hers, they were moving up and down, a tender caress of roughened and exciting flesh against her bare arms. "I can tend to be a very private person," he was saying. "I think I'm a man who needs to be close to a woman before he really tells her his thoughts and . . . activities."

"I didn't mean to pry," Brittany murmured. She swallowed, fascinated by the pulse against his throat. She tilted back her head and gave him a soft but dazzling smile. "I just wanted to know more about you."

"And I didn't mean to imply that you were prying. Only that I want to know more about you, too."

She just kept smiling. There was something . . . something in the husky tone of his voice that made her think that they were fencing; that they were both players in a game of deceit. And perhaps they were. But then, as she watched him, and as he touched her, all the undercurrents changed.

His hands were on her shoulders, and as he leaned toward her, she knew he intended to kiss her. And she knew what kind of a kiss it would be. A light touch; a gentle, physical contact that would be like a slow, rippling wave that came before the sweep of a tide. She would welcome that contact; she had planned on it. And as she watched his features, tense now, his eyes a smoky shade to match the coming dusk, she thought with a little thrill of triumph that she could succeed at a reckless game. She could eventually draw him out and prove beyond a doubt his guilt or innocence. Perhaps she was playing with fire, but her heartache decreed that she must take the chance of being singed, that she would play against all odds.

But when his lips touched hers, all that was meant to be was gone. It was a gentle touch, infinitely tender. It warmed, warmed and deepened; cunning and deceit faded into the pink and gray of the encroaching twilight. Brittany felt his strong arms around her, she felt his tongue rimming her mouth, her lips parting to accept him. She breathed and her body filled with the scent of him, clean and unique. She wanted him; she wanted to come closer and closer to him, and the sweetness of that touch overwhelmed all else. Her arms curled about his neck, she arched to his length. And each sensation was all the more sweet. The liquid warmth and searching pressure of his mouth . . . his tongue, the hardness of his hips, the muscled breadth of his chest, crushing so solidly against her breasts. It was that feeling again; not that he was a man who needed to conquer, but that he could bring out all that was best in a woman, bring her soaring with him to heights of reckless excitement and breathless abandon.

She didn't care where they were; the gardens eclipsed them from view of the house, but it wouldn't have mattered. Something had gone astray; she had melted into that kiss, savoring all that her senses gave her, memorizing him in the way that a lover did: the feel of his cheek against her palm; the heat of his body, giving hers fever; the pressure of his hips, the hardness of his thighs. His fingers laced through her hair—exploring, as she explored. And his mouth. So tender upon hers that it was more intimate in itself than she had ever imagined. Finally . . . reluctantly, pulling away.

And then his eyes, meeting hers again, telling her in those first brief seconds that it had all been as spontaneous with him as it had with her. And as Brittany returned his stare, searching out his eyes, it dawned on her that she had committed the gravest sin: she had betrayed herself. She had been willing to go to great lengths to gain his trust, but she hadn't intended to lose her own soul.

Darkness came suddenly. It fell about them like a curtain of mist and smoke, and like a curtain, it created a barrier between them. She saw his eyes change; no longer bared to hers, they were gray, darkened by the night that was with them at last, their only glitter that of a diamond-hard shield. But his touch . . . he didn't turn that to a lie. He didn't release her. And when he spoke, the burr was rich in his words, and they were soft.

"We'd better return to the house. We're due at dinner very soon, I imagine."

"Yes."

He took her hand. Brittany was silent as he led the way back to the house.

The lights were coming on as they neared the *casa*. In the courtyard, the cascading fountains were caught in sparkling brilliance: it was as if the *casa* had found a new and even more glorious life with darkness and the night. It was illusion, Brit-

67

tany warned herself; day transformed into night, and she became captive in the twilight.

Twilight . . . because she didn't know what was right, and what was wrong. She was barely even aware that she was praying again.

Don't let it be him. Please, don't let it be him.

In the patio, he turned to her. "Would you do me a favor tonight, please?"

"What?" They sounded so normal.

His smile was back. The one that was subtly amused, yet somehow warm. The one that held a borderline of warmth—and danger.

"Wear the silk tonight."

"The silk?"

"The emerald silk. For me."

Take a step backward, Brittany, she warned herself. A giant step backward. She had been worrying about her dress for the affair; wondering if any of her own gowns would be up to par for the occasion. It was almost as if he knew . . . and was giving her an easy out.

"Surely," she told him softly, and she managed to retain her smile until she had turned, and hurried down the corridor.

Flynn noted that his tux had been laid out on the bed. White tails, white vest, black bow tie. Damn, but Donald was bloody proper. Always correct.

He grimaced. What would he do without Donald?

He stripped off his shoes, then his shirt, and then, by long habit, pulled off his watch and set it on the dresser. He paused, listening. He could hear the muted sound of running water.

Flynn wondered briefly if Brittany was aware that her room was directly next to his. She would be taking a shower—or a

68

bath. One way or another, she would be stepping into the water. Naked. He already knew a fair amount of her form. She had been in a wisp of a bikini when he had pulled her from the water. He knew that she was slim and beautifully tanned; he knew that her hips curved nicely and that her breasts were full and firm. And he had touched her and held her close and he knew that her compact form had the added attraction of warmth and passion and supple vitality . . .

Flynn gave himself a little shake. He was still standing before his dresser, as if frozen in motion. His watch still dangled in his hand.

What are you doing? he asked himself in dismay, slipping out of his trousers and briefs and striding into his own bath. He paused before the mirror and ran a hand over his cheeks. Yeah, he needed a shave. He'd shower first.

Once inside the shower, he tried to allow himself to assess the situation with an objective mind. It was evident that she was playing a game; that was all right—he knew how to survive at the game. Once he figured out what it was.

But down by the beach . . . for those few minutes, he could have believed everything that she seemed—even knowing that she was a liar. When he had held her, he had known a warmth he hadn't felt in years, a burning desire to make it all real. He had wanted to accept every word that she said, to allow her beneath his skin, and into his heart.

Bewitched, he warned himself. You pulled a siren from the sea, and you're willing to suspend the truth for magic. She's good, that's all. Brilliant at her act. And it is an act, because you know too many truths . . .

Something in him protested that the haunting exchange of warmth and fire at the beach couldn't have been a lie. Neither of them had expected the chemistry, the ease with which they had come together. Even now it was a memory that could haunt and tease, cause him to tremble inside with the desire to touch her again, and follow the path still farther.

"Ego," he chastised himself aloud, and the riveting water of the shower seemed to echo the word. You want it to be so, and so you will convince yourself that it is . . .

He couldn't. He had thought himself the hunter; it was hard to accept that he was the hunted. He was suddenly vulnerable to eyes of green fire and a voice that touched him like a brush of silk.

Flynn stepped closer to the spigot and rubbed his face strenuously while the water pounded into it. He couldn't afford any slipups. Things were coming to a head; a few more takes, and he could be done with the long haul. Take a vacation, a break. Reap the satisfactions and rewards of his labors.

She could be useful. If he moved right, he could use her to draw out the others. She was beautiful, elegant, and perfect. No one but he would ever suspect her . . .

He pulled away from the shower and soaped himself vigorously. He wasn't really afraid of her, or afraid that she could really get in his way. He had a fair amount of confidence in his abilities, simply because he had been at it all so long. There was still something that bothered him; like a flaw he couldn't see, something that was there, but just couldn't be touched . . .

Flynn paused again, feeling the rush of the water full force. Steam was rising all around him.

He understood the feeling that had eluded him.

Yes, he wanted to sit back. He wanted to take a break. To spend time at honest leisure, not searching, not watching; just sitting back and truly seeing a sunset, the ocean beneath a crimson sky, enjoying the cool whisper of the wind or the warm caress of a fire against the cold . . .

He didn't want to do it alone.

Once, he had come to believe that love itself was an illusion, that nothing of beauty could last. He had been young then, hurt and brash. The years had dimmed that pain; he looked back with only a little wistful sadness at what had been —what might have been had either he or Barbara possessed any wisdom—but was lost in the folly of temper and youth instead.

It was all long, long gone. And it had never come again— that feeling of urgency and need, longing to touch and be touched, to share the good and the bad, innermost thoughts and the most idle laughter.

And yet this girl with the emerald eyes . . .

It wasn't love, and it wasn't lust. Well, maybe there was just a little lust involved—he'd be a fool or a blind man not to be feeling a little lust. He was drawn to her. Pulled closer and closer by the tenacious threads of fascination. The hint of something deep and binding; summer days touched by the sea and sun, long winter nights warmed by a fire. Waking each morning beside a lovely and loved face with lips that curled to a shell-pink smile . . .

There was enough steam in the bathroom for him to call it a sauna.

Flynn gave himself an impatient shake. He hadn't survived it all thus far by falling prey to beautiful faces.

He knew damned well that she was a liar. He couldn't allow himself to forget for a minute just how adept she was at her lies. He had to accept them all . . .

He just couldn't fall for them. Or her.

Until his day came to get at the truth. Which it would, he assured himself. Soon enough.

CHAPTER FOUR

Flynn's car was a sporty Porsche, a red convertible. He asked Brittany if she minded driving with the top down. She assured him that she didn't, silently glad that she had given up on the idea of doing something elegant with her hair, and had just left it to swing loose down her back.

The night was lovely and exciting. Lights sparkled upon the water; the air smelled pleasantly of salt and freshness and as the little car whipped along, Brittany felt soothed at the rush of wind against her cheeks. Flynn was a competent driver; she felt comfortable leaning back in the seat and allowing herself to feel the soft touch of the dark sky and delightful brush of the night air. Occasionally he glanced her way, and she was able to give him a languorous smile that bespoke a total ease with his company.

At length he turned inland, and they began to climb from sea level. The wind still caught at locks of her hair and teased them about her face, but Flynn slowed their speed, and they were able to talk above the roar of the engine.

"How large a gathering is it going to be?" she asked him. Her eyes fell to his hands, dark against the beige leather covering on the wheel and the snow white of his tux. A trembling sensation took her unaware as she suddenly remembered being in his arms; feeling those hands at her nape, coursing along her spine . . .

"Not too large, from what I understand," Flynn responded, flashing her a white smile. "Juan will be there. You and I, Ian, Mr. and Mrs. St. John, Joshua and his wife and their daughter, and Rose."

Brittany caught a flying wave of hair and twisted the whole of its length into a knot with her fingers as she turned to him with a laugh. "You're forgetting I'm new here. Ian is our host, I know. Who are the others? I'm afraid I'm going to be a bit of an outsider."

"Oh, I doubt that," Flynn assured her, giving her a quick glance that appeared almost sardonic in the play of moon glow and shadow. "I've a feeling you'll be quite the rage of the ball, so to say." He gave her no chance to protest or comment, but continued, "There's a bit of a social system here, you see. A number of Britons, a few Americans . . ." He shrugged. "It seems sometimes—in Spain—that we become one with a common language. Each season, there's a regular scurry of events. A closed group in a way." He gave her a wide grin that was ruefully honest. "Edith St. John reigns as queen. She's from Coventry; Harry, her husband, is an American. He's a middle-aged man, meek beside our *grande dame,* and yet his witticisms fly right over her busy head. You'll enjoy them. She's a whirlwind and a bit of a busybody, but her heart is really one of brilliant silver, if not gold. Josh and his wife are the newcomers; they just took up residence here last Christmas with Elly—Eleanor, their daughter. She's eighteen, I believe, sometimes sweet, sometimes rebellious but very pretty and nice. The Joneses are thoroughly pleasant—and Edith's a delight. Carrie Jones is the granddaughter of an earl, you see. Josh has the Midas touch, so they're also the most fascinatingly affluent of our group."

Brittany smiled at him as he glanced her way, then turned her gaze to the winding road before them. She had felt a touch of electric warmth when their eyes had met. He liked the people he was talking about; they were his friends. He could comment on their foibles with no rancor, but with a gentle humor, and she felt that he included himself when he wryly mocked the social stratum in which he moved. And she liked that about him; she sensed that she would understand all that he had said when she met these people, and that she would meet his eyes again later that evening and know that he was sending a silent message. "See, I told you that we were all a bit off the wall!"

And she would understand. She would smile because it would be so nice to be on the same wavelength, so nice to share that unspoken communication.

Danger zone, Brittany, she warned herself. It was startling to learn that she was to meet her third quarry that evening— Joshua Jones—as well as Ian Drury. She had been wondering how to approach Jones. A little frown formed between her eyes. Jones was married to the granddaughter of an earl. He had a Midas touch. He didn't sound like the type of man who would embezzle from little old ladies. But then neither did Flynn. Not Flynn. But Flynn *was* guilty of lying . . .

"And what is Ian like?"

"Charming I suppose," Flynn said with a noncommittal shrug. "He throws good parties."

He wasn't looking at her, so she couldn't begin to read his expression. There didn't seem to be any hostility to his tone, it was pleasant and casual enough . . . maybe just a shade more tense than it had been before?

Brittany waited a minute, but he wasn't going to say any more. "And who is Rose?" she prompted at last.

Damn, if he didn't smile! Slowly, a lazy grin just curling

pleasantly into the line of his lips. "Rose," he murmured, and she sensed his affection for the woman from the warmth of his tone.

"Is she English?" Brittany prompted when it appeared that he had forgotten to answer her, being too absorbed in his own reflections. Brittany was annoyed, then irritated—because she had felt herself becoming so annoyed.

"Rosy?" He queried, glancing her way. "No, Rosy is very much a Spaniard. Young and wild and very impetuous. A lot of fun. You'll like her."

Will I? Brittany wondered. And then she was horrified to realize that jealousy was creeping into her system. Dear Lord, she couldn't be jealous. She couldn't allow this man to mean anything to her . . .

"There's Ian's house now. You can just see his *casa* through the trees."

Brittany caught sight of the sprawling white structure through dark and spidery branches. It was one-storied, with an elaborate and porticoed entryway. If Ian Drury's *casa* hadn't been impressive by sheer size, its entry—with the five towering columns and foliaged, sweeping drive—would have earned a gasp of admiration on its own.

"It's marvelous," Brittany murmured.

"You like it better than mine?" He was gazing her way, eyes sparkling, deep blue and jet, and a brow raised teasingly.

"Oh, no," Brittany responded lightly in kind. "Your *casa* has much more character."

It did. It housed *his* character.

Flynn chuckled softly, enjoying her response. "Let's hope you still feel that way when the evening's over," he murmured.

The car passed by an iron gate; Flynn waved to the guard on duty, and the guard—apparently accustomed to his car—

waved in return. They began a slight ascent; the house wasn't really on a hill, it was just elevated. The drive curved gracefully through a myriad of tall and flowered bushes and then the lighted entryway seemed to burst upon them. Flynn drove beneath the portico. Before he had brought the car to a halt, two men attired in dark suits were at both doors, opening them politely.

"*Buenas noches*, Señor Flynn," they seemed to chorus.

White-gloved hands helped Brittany to the tiled walk. "*Buenas noches*, Roberto, Alfredo." He tossed his keys to the dark young man he had addressed as Roberto. "This is Señorita Martin; I'm sure you'll be seeing her again."

Pleasant, mumbled Spanish came her way. Brittany murmured something in return, then Flynn was taking her arm to lead her to the house.

The front door was opened. Another man in a black tux was there to greet them. "Señor Colby—it is good to see you. Señor Drury was growing anxious."

"We are a little late, aren't we, Oliver?" Flynn smiled and again turned to Brittany. "Brittany, Oliver. Should you ever need anything while at Ian's home, Oliver is the man to see. Oliver, I would like you to meet Ms. Brittany Martin. I believe —if we're lucky—she'll be with us for the summer."

"Ms. Martin, I am at your service." Oliver bowed to her. He was an Englishman, very tall and straight, with iron-gray hair.

"Thank you, Oliver," Brittany said. He nodded and stepped aside.

Flynn led Brittany onward through the foyer. There were plants everywhere, it seemed, vines and flowers, curling around a grillwork that lined the walls. The foyer was larger than her entire house in Florida.

Brittany felt the touch of Flynn's warm whisper against her ear. "And now, my love, you are about to face the lions."

She glanced his way quickly. He was smiling, but he was watching her curiously. She returned his smile. "Lions? They'll be lovely, I'm certain."

His secretive smile remained curled in place. Brittany heard light, pattering footsteps hurrying up a pair of stairs that seemed to lead to a sunken grand room beyond the grill.

"Flynn! You come up with a mermaid, and we're all just dying of curiosity to meet her, and you make your appearance late. How rude! But then you never did really stand by ceremony, did you, darling?"

The footsteps—and the soft, sultry voice belonged to one of the most lovely women Brittany had ever seen. She was elegantly tall, elegantly slim—but very curvacious. Her hair was ebony black, free about one shoulder, caught back against the other ear by a blood-red flower. Her gown was not low cut, just slashed to give the advantage to that one bare shoulder. Her eyes, like her hair, appeared to be jet; her face was shaped much like a heart, the lines beautiful, the skin golden and beautifully clear. Her mouth was a bow, generous and full and red, and her smile was deep and genuine.

Flynn was returning her affectionate gaze. Brittany suddenly felt short; she had been confident about her gown and appearance, but now that confidence seemed to be ebbing away.

"Rose . . . hello." Flynn took both her hands, and kissed her cheek. They knew each other very well, Brittany decided, withdrawing defensively to a position of objectivity. She was here to watch and to learn . . . to catch a thief.

Neither of them was rude; they both turned to her immediately. "Rose, I'd like you to meet my mermaid. Miss Brittany—"

77

"Martin, of the United States," Rose interrupted and finished, offering Brittany a hand that was long-fingered, longer nailed, and bedecked with a massive sapphire, fine gold bands, and even tiny studs of diamond chips set into each long nail. But her touch was a firm one; the handshake as warm as her smile. "Brittany, I'm Rose Montelbello and it's a true pleasure to welcome you!"

"Thank you," Brittany murmured. Rose gave Flynn a wry glance and slipped an arm through Brittany's, leading her on ahead. "That he pulled you from the sea, how exciting! You must tell me all about it at dinner. I had my own escapade with El Drago, did you know?"

"No—" Brittany began, trying to follow Rose's quick, softly accented speech. Uneasiness settled over her. Rose had encountered El Drago? Why hadn't Flynn mentioned it?

And just what was his relationship with Rose? Their ease with one another was disturbing. It was as if they shared a communication. The kind of communication that was exchanged between an attractive man and equally attractive woman . . . who were lovers.

"We'll talk at dinner, yes? Now you must meet the rest . . . oh, you know Juan, don't you?"

"Yes—"

"But Ian—he is most anxious!"

Well, so far, she hadn't been called on much for conversation, Brittany decided. Rose managed to carry that ball, delightfully. It was strange—but safe—Brittany decided.

But for how long?

Rose was proceeding down that short flight of stairs; Brittany heard Flynn following quietly behind them. Then they were in the massive grand room, and she was seeing everyone at once—and nervously wondering just where her problems would lie.

"Everyone!" Rose called out gaily. "Flynn has arrived at last—and brought us Ms. Martin. Brittany—that tall handsome hombre by the mantel is our host, Ian Drury. You know Juan, of course. There's Edith St. John and her husband Harry; the lovely blonde is Elly Jones, and on her left, Joshua and Carrie."

"Welcome!" Harry St. John said quietly, raising a glass to greet her. Juan was smiling lackadaisically. Elly Jones *was* a pretty blonde who nodded but seemed a bit sullen. Joshua Jones—slender and gray haired—echoed Harry's welcome, and his wife murmured, "What a pleasure" very sweetly.

Edith and Ian came toward her at the same time; Edith seemed to chug along like a barge on a river. She was endowed with a massive bosom, pure silver hair, and huge, sparkling eyes that took note of the world, refusing to apologize for healthy curiosity.

Ian—a very handsome hombre indeed—moved more with the grace of a cat, accepting indulgently Edith's charge of affairs, and politely awaiting a chance to greet his guest.

"Ms. Martin!" Edith St. John took both her hands. "An American, how lovely. And you poor dear! You mustn't worry about a thing at all. If Flynn becomes too mysterious—or chauvinistic!—for your liking, you're more than welcome to move right in with us. I understand your parents are about Europe somewhere. You'll have to tell me about them. Harry is an American—we're quite familiar with some of *the* families." The inflection was light, but it was there.

"Flynn has been a perfect gentleman, Mrs. St. John, but I do thank you sincerely for the invitation," Brittany said. She heard her own words, and breathed easily. She sounded fine, relaxed. She could—unless disaster struck in a mysterious way—make her way through the evening fine.

Rose laughed from somewhere nearby, a soft, husky and

delightful sound. "Flynn! Well, hombre, it is good to hear that you have been on your best behavior. I've many good things to say of my dear friend, but . . ."

Brittany turned to see that Rose and Flynn were smiling affectionately at one another again. The sparkle was in Flynn's eyes; Rose's words did not offend him, they amused him.

Rose turned from Flynn to Brittany. "I do not always call him a gentleman. But then, I do not like my men too gentle."

"Ah, but Rose, you bring out the hungering beast in all of us," Flynn returned, and it seemed that everyone laughed, because she was, of course, so very stunning, and it was probably true.

"Rosy, you also bring out our very best," Ian Drury said gallantly, stepping past Edith at last with a smile. He, too, took Brittany's hands and pulled them close to his chest as he stared down into her eyes.

Gallant words, Brittany thought, but this was a man on the move. His eyes were a tawny color; he *was* very handsome. A bit shorter than Flynn, and it seemed, a bit broader. He might have been a tackle for the L.A. Raiders. His face was broad where Flynn's tended to be gaunt; his hair was not quite so richly dark, yet both men could most definitely fit the bill of "charming." But it was the look in those tawny eyes that caught Brittany's attention. He *did* like women.

"Ms. Martin, since I first heard the story, I was aching with envy for my friend Flynn. That *he* was the one to take you from the sea."

Brittany returned his charismatic grin, and allowed her hands to linger in his grip. "How charming, Mr. Drury," she returned sweetly.

A hand slipped around her elbow; strangely she knew the touch even before she turned, taken subtly but cleanly from

Ian's grasp. Flynn . . . there was power in his hold, and tension.

"Ian, be a good chap and fix your guests a drink, will you?"

Ian shrugged. "But of course. Brittany? I may use your given name, I hope?"

"Of course . . ."

"Flynn is a Scotch drinker—I think the Scottish have to drink Scotch—patriotism or something like that. But what is your pleasure?"

"She's fond of decent wine," Flynn replied, before Brittany could answer. She thought his tone was a little dry—and also, that there was an edge to it.

"Wine, Brittany?" Ian inquired.

Not if it tastes like that horrible Riesling, Brittany thought, but she must have nodded, or perhaps people were just accustomed to accepting Flynn's words, because Ian was headed to a glass and chrome buffet to pour her wine.

Flynn continued to hold her arm. They followed along behind Ian. "You're from Florida, Brittany," Ian was saying. He turned to hand her a fluted glass. "You must be accustomed to our heat."

Brittany accepted the glass. "Yes, but the evenings are different here—quite cool."

"Umm sometimes," Ian murmured. "Have you been to the Costa del Sol before? No, I think not. We would have found you before . . . one of us would have, certainly."

"Most certainly," Edith St. John murmured indignantly. "And to think that the poor child arrives and is immediately approached by that horrid pirate—"

"Oh, not so horrid, I wouldn't think," her husband offered levelly. "In fact, my dear, I think that you're rather insulted that the gallant rake hasn't approached you yet." His wife gave him a gaze that might have sliced steel; Harry was unperturbed, but he smiled and amended his statement. "You're such an adventurous woman, love—I'm sure you'd be happy to give El Drago a sound piece of your mind."

"Yes, dear, yes, I suppose you're right," Edith murmured, her ruffled feathers smoothed. "I would dearly love to give that rake a piece of my mind!"

Oliver appeared at the steps, clearing his throat. "If it's agreeable, Mr. Drury, dinner will be served."

Ian Drury lifted a brow and surveyed his guests. His eyes came to rest upon Brittany, and he might have been speaking to her alone. "Is it agreeable . . . ?"

There was a murmur of assent. Flynn was still behind Brittany, actually touching her, brushing against her. But Ian moved smoothly, taking her opposite elbow. As the host, it was obviously his position to lead them all to the dining room.

"I insist upon the pleasure of seating you beside me, Brittany," he murmured. Brittany politely agreed, but she spoke softly, trying to keep an ear open to the conversations going on behind her. Joshua Jones seemed to be having a controlled disagreement with his pretty—but presently sullen—daughter. Edith was still telling her husband what she would say to El Drago. Juan was apparently escorting Carrie Jones and Flynn . . .

Flynn was murmuring something to Rose in soft and velvet tones that were filled with the warm cadence of his native burr. Rose was laughing.

The seating for dinner couldn't have given Brittany a better opportunity to observe those she needed to know. Ian was to her left; Joshua Jones to her right. Elly was to Ian's left, and lovely Rose was seated across the table, beside Flynn.

Flynn seemed to have the talent to enjoy the camaraderie of the woman beside him while also keeping a disturbingly astute eye on Brittany. She gripped her hands tightly together in her lap for a minute, and breathed deeply. He could stare all he cared to. She was going to be sweet and charming and breeze through the evening and she was going to do all that she had set out to do.

Conversation was light at first, as palatable as the decorative fruit cup that was served them. Joshua Jones talked about a particular form of Spanish sculpture that he thought would do brilliantly well at his English gallery. Brittany gave him her avid attention, and all that she saw of the man puzzled her. He spoke with a quiet voice; he seemed the epitome of that elusive being the "true gentleman." He also seemed to be a troubled man. His eyes often fell on his daughter, who didn't offer him even a façade of polite attention. She ignored him, and played with a piece of avocado in her fruit cup.

Over a chilled tomato bisque, Ian and Flynn turned the conversation to polo ponies.

"Do you enjoy the game, Brittany?" Ian asked her.

Flynn saved her from an answer. "Brittany is not fond of horses, Ian."

"Oh, what a pity. Perhaps we could get her to enjoy the sport from the sidelines."

"I intend to do all that I can," Flynn said, and Brittany felt his stare very keenly.

She smiled winningly at both men. "I suppose that anything is possible."

She didn't find herself in the least on the hook until the entrée came, spiced and tender steaks. It was just when she'd taken a bite of her delicious meat that she was jolted away from the possibility of enjoying anything else that might be served.

Rose—innocently, Brittany believed—was the one to drop the bombshell.

"Brittany, you must tell us more about your encounter with El Drago. We were ever so surprised."

"Uh . . . why?" she managed to swallow and ask.

"Well, simply because he's . . . well, one does not use the word 'charming' to describe a pirate, does she? But until now he has never really threatened anyone. He is more of a . . . Flynn! What is the name I am looking for?"

"Robin Hood?" Flynn suggested. Damn him. Those eyes of his really seemed to be cutting into Brittany. She fixed her own gaze on Rose.

"Yes—yes, a Robin Hood!" Rose lightly clapped her hands together, pleased that her frustration for words was at an end. "To the Spanish, at least, you see. It seems that he only attacks the English."

"The English," Brittany echoed. "But I don't understand. You just told me that he attacked you, and you are a Spaniard."

"Sí, sí," Rose said impatiently, "but I was on one of Ian's ketches that day. El Drago stripped down the boat—oh, he was efficient! He took everything. But he apologized to me; he said that he did not wish to cause me fear or distress. He kissed my hand, and when he was through with the ketch, he gave me a rose."

Ian muttered a soft, impatient oath. "Rosa! It sounds as if you were taken with the man. Women! It seems they love a scoundrel every time. They are always taken in by the flash of a smile!"

"They do say," Juan offered from the other end of the table with an amused grin, "that there is something . . . sensual about a cordial thief. Think of it! Poor Rose. All alone in the blackguard's clutches; she is vulnerable to him. But he . . . he treats her like the lady she is and *voilà*—you have it. A man whose power becomes almost . . . sexual."

Rose had been listening to Juan with amusement. She didn't demur, but laughed good-naturedly. "Perhaps I *was* a bit taken by the man." She stared at Brittany. "I didn't really see him, you know; it was becoming night and there was so much darkness. But there was much life to him . . ." She turned to stare down at Juan. "Yes, *mi amigo*, he was sexy. I thought so then . . . but I'm not so sure now. Not since I've heard of his rude attack upon Brittany. He was so threatening to you, then?"

Why the hell, Brittany wondered, hadn't some enterprising young journalist thought to play up the charm of this pirate in the papers? It would have made a great story—and it would have given her some decent warning.

She swallowed some of the burgundy, which had been served with the steaks, to play for time. Then she set her glass down, and smiled ruefully—aware now that all eyes from around the table were fixed on her. Even those of the sullen Miss Elly Jones.

"Perhaps he never had a chance to be cordial. I was in absolute panic. I started screaming and thrashing—and handling it all very poorly—from the very beginning."

"Yes, perhaps *you* threatened *him*," Flynn said politely. She couldn't read a thing from the opaque smoke of his eyes. "It's possible that your behavior actually frightened him from his customary act."

"Yes! That could be!" Rose said excitedly, as if they had just solved a great mystery. And it seemed those at the table thought the explanation a good one, and so Brittany was relieved.

"Well," Ian said disgustedly, inadvertently giving Brittany another out, "I think this pirate is an obnoxious menace, and I'd just as soon not have him discussed at my dinner table. The man has cost me a small fortune."

85

"He is a horrid creature!" Elly Jones exclaimed, breaking what had hitherto been an absolute silence on her part. "Any time Ian's men take his ships to sea, they are crudely attacked —and they don't receive roses!"

Ian gazed fondly at Elly. "Please, you needn't worry so for me, my dear. It's just an annoyance, nothing more. One day I shall tackle the man myself, and his days of grandeur will reach a crude end!"

"I wonder why you haven't run into him yet, Ian." Joshua Jones asked, puzzled.

"Perhaps," Flynn murmured, "it's because Ian hasn't been out on the sea much himself lately. Have you, Ian?"

"I've been busy with other things," Ian murmured. He gazed at Flynn. "One of those new horses I was telling you about. I just had him brought from England, traveled with him myself, I did. You'll want to see him after dinner, I assume."

"Of course," Flynn said, and the conversation turned back to polo once again, with Edith boisterously—and Carrie Jones more quietly—telling Brittany just how much she was missing by not enjoying the polo scene.

Brittany seemed to be in the clear for the rest of the meal. She might have enjoyed the food once again, except for the sensation that kept rippling heatedly through her.

A sensation of being watched.

But then she *was* being watched. By Flynn. She could feel the touch of his blue fire-and-smoke eyes.

And that was why the rippling sensation seemed to be such a very warm one . . .

When the meal was over, aperitifs were served out by the pool. The men were still talking polo; Ian suggested that those who cared to might come to the stable and see his new stallion. Flynn readily agreed. Brittany assumed that she would come along, until Elly Jones declined. Brittany then said that she would stay behind too.

Elly did not particularly appear to appreciate the gesture, but Brittany felt that she needed a break from being constantly on guard, and Elly Jones was the daughter of Joshua Jones. Perhaps Brittany could learn more about the man from the girl than she could from trying to delicately quiz *him*.

When the others left, Brittany walked idly along the length of the pool. Elly made no move to draw her into conversation, so Brittany moved back to Elly and perched beside her on one of the wicker chairs that sat beneath the gazebo. "You haven't been at Costa del Sol long yourself, have you?" Brittany asked her with a friendly smile.

"No," Elly responded, not looking at her. Then she swallowed a bit guiltily and apologized. "I am sorry; I don't mean to be so rude. I—I guess I should admit that I hate it here. I loved our home in London. My Spanish is horrible, and I—I just hate it." She smiled wistfully and warmly then and said vehemently, "Thank God for Ian! He's just so lovely—he's made it bearable here!"

Brittany smiled, feeling sorry for the girl. She was very young, and apparently very lonely. And it seemed she was setting herself up for a bit of heartache, because Ian didn't appear to be the man to return such ardent loyalty to one woman.

"Don't you get back to England now and then?"

Elly sniffed. "No. Father goes. He was there just recently. But it was 'business'—and I wasn't allowed along. He's such a frightful bore! Everyone claims that my father is so bright and wonderful, but I don't think he's so terribly clever. We should be totally comfortable, but he's continually tying up our finances. He's always complaining that I spend so much, and that I must stop thinking I can hop from country to country at whim. And then I'm stuck here in this alien place with only . . ."

Elly shot Brittany another quick glance. "I'm so sorry again. I shouldn't be telling you all this."

"It's fine, really, Elly. I don't intend to say a word to anyone."

Elly sighed, leaned back in her chair, and closed her eyes. "You seem so kind . . . I never have anyone to talk to anymore."

Brittany watched the girl, and her heart ached a little again. Being young was difficult. Elly seemed like a very delicate flower with her sun-gold hair, rosy complexion, and cornflower eyes. A frown disturbed her brow now, even in relaxation.

She was evidently champing at the bit to become an adult.

"Well, you can talk to me any time you like," Brittany murmured cheerfully. "I'd like some company myself while I'm here."

Elly opened a single eye. "But you've got Flynn, then, don't you?"

"Got him?" Brittany repeated with a laugh. "No—I'm just relying upon his hospitality until I . . ." She paused. It seemed such a sin to lie to Elly. But Elly was Joshua's daughter, and from her words, Joshua was beginning to appear more and more suspicious.

"I'm just staying with Flynn until I can contact someone and get my life sewn back together!"

Elly closed her eye again and smiled. "Flynn is great. I was halfway in love with him for a while except—" She opened her eyes and grinned ruefully. "—except that he's kind to girls my age, and nothing more! I was a bit crushed at first, but he turned out to be such a friend. If only he would quit telling me to understand my father—and not be in such a rush to grow up. I have grown up! I'd leave home, but . . ."

"But what?"

"My grandfather was the Earl of Claremont and he left me a marvelous trust—I just can't touch it until my twenty-first birthday. And so I'm stuck!"

Brittany smiled. "It won't really be all that long, Elly. And really, we all do make mistakes when we're young. Especially with our love lives."

"Have you made mistakes?"

"Sure. As I said—we all do." Brittany wasn't about to offer any more.

"If only I were an American!" Elly moaned.

"I don't think it would change the frustration," Brittany told her wryly. But she noticed that Elly was no longer paying any attention to her. Elly's eyes were fixed on the trail that led to the stables out back, and there was a tender glow to them.

Ian Drury was leading the others back to the pool area. Rose had an arm linked with his—and with Flynn's. They appeared to be a cordial threesome.

"I feel like dancing, Ian!" Rose was saying. "The night is so young and alive! Music, my host! We must have some music, so that the night can live on!"

Ian agreed and called Oliver, and soon the pool and patio were filled with the sounds of keyboards and guitars; Spanish crooners and American and British top forty tunes.

Rose danced her way over to Brittany and Elly, laughing with good humor. "Surely, as an American, Brittany Martin, you dance! Of course, they do say, though, that it is Latins who come alive with music. Elly—you will dance, yes?"

"Oh, yes, I love to dance," Elly responded.

Brittany smiled at Rose, then watched Elly again. Elly hadn't taken her eyes from Ian, who was then approaching them. She could almost feel the young girl's heartbeat, and a glance at Rose assured Brittany that the Spanish woman was both aware of and bemused by Elly's obvious infatuation with their host.

Rose looked like a woman who had experienced all the follies of youth—and learned a great deal. Brittany couldn't deny Rose's intimacy with Flynn was more disturbing to her than she would have liked it to be, but the more she saw of Rose, the more she liked her.

"I love to dance," Elly murmured again, but when Ian reached their group, he did not seem to notice her words—or the pleading adoration in her eyes.

He stretched out a hand to Brittany, pulling her to her feet before she could demur.

"Come, Ms. Martin, into my arms for one sweep around the patio before your rescuer can whisk you away from me!"

The music was slow and soft and Spanish, pulsing with sensuality. She was locked in his arms, twirling, aware of his handsome features close to hers. And yet as they spun her gaze moved, too; she saw quick images of those around them.

Elly, staring at her, her pretty face pinched with hurt; Joshua Jones, watching his daughter with irritation . . . and Ian with hostility. Brittany saw Edith, lecturing to Juan, Carrie Jones, and Harry St. Clare. She saw Rose—just observing.

And she saw Flynn. Staring at her, watching her, his eyes not blue now, but slate gray, narrowed. He looked angry, tense, and irritated. And yet, when he caught her eyes on him, he smiled and waved.

Brittany lifted a hand from Ian's shoulder in return. She smiled, and yet she shivered, because she felt the smile that she had been offered hadn't been sincere in the least. Only the tension had been real.

"Are you with me at all, Brittany?" Ian queried her.

"Oh, yes, of course!" She pulled back slightly and gave Ian a merry laugh.

She had to ignore Flynn. She wanted to talk to Ian. Draw him out and discover what she could.

But over his shoulder she could see Flynn. He was talking to Juan now; Edith St. John was dancing with her husband. Flynn was *listening* to Juan rather, she decided. But he was still watching her. Eyes still narrowed, yet now they seemed to hold a silver glitter and when he smiled again, she felt a trembling within her. It was a damned dangerous smile. One just like the cat might give the canary before . . .

"Ah, Ms. Martin," Ian murmured to her. "Where have you been all my life? What have you been doing?"

"Floating around the sea," Brittany teased in return. But her thoughts were running a different course.

I just want to know *where you've been* and *what you've been doing* for the *last two weeks*, Mr. Drury.

"Here comes the Scottish thorn in my side!" Ian groaned. "Ah, well, the Scots have always been a thorn to the English —I'll just have to persevere as my countrymen are wont to do. You and I need to be alone some time."

"Soon," Brittany agreed sweetly.

And then Flynn was there, cutting in—politely. But as soon as he touched Brittany she felt his heat and tension . . . and the anger in him that belied his cordial words.

His eyes were a stormy sea; his expression brooded like thunder. Brittany tensed, whirling close to him, feeling their bodies crush together with the sensual pulse of the music. She fanned her lashes over her cheeks, preparing to defend herself, issuing mental warnings that she must be sweet and innocent no matter what he said. Her nails scraped lightly over the fabric of his tux; she opened her eyes to his.

And she trembled again; not with fear, but with something

91

akin to it. Ian was an attractive man, very appealing. But being held by Flynn . . . was lightning! His vibrancy touched and enthralled her. And his eyes . . .

Was it anger? Because he smiled again. Why didn't she feel his humor, the touch of warmth to his laughter and his eyes? But he had no rebuke to give her; his words were velvet, a breath against her cheek. "You are enjoying yourself, I hope, Brittany."

"Yes. Are you?"

"If you're happy, so am I."

He moved fluently; he led her into a turn, and her cheek crushed against his tux. The material teased her; she felt the pulse of his heart along with the music, and she could no longer see his eyes. What, she wondered a little desperately, was he really thinking? There was no way to know. The music changed to a spirited flamenco number and they broke apart; all spells were broken because Rose had the floor.

Beautiful, lively, sensual, she was entertaining them all with her graceful dance. Her eyes touched Ian's and Flynn's, and Brittany was curiously jealous again, aware that Rose was unique; she combined passion with sophistication, pleasantry with wisdom.

She knew Flynn very, very well.

When the number ended, Rose tossed back her head. Her magnificent hair fell like an ebony waterfall down her back. But as applause greeted her performance, she laughed dismissively, and then she was declaring that it was far later than she had thought. Juan sprang forward to tell her he would take her home, and the party began to break up.

Brittany realized that she was very tired. It seemed that she had carried the evening off. Invitations cascaded upon her ears from the Joneses and the St. Johns—and from Ian. She was so tired that they seemed to spin in her head. But it didn't matter. Flynn answered for her. "Just call . . . Brittany will be there."

But when his eyes touched hers again—crystal ice—she felt that sense of danger. It was also in his touch, light as he took her arm, but laced with electricity.

She closed her eyes once they were in the Porsche, leaning back against the seat. Yet she was so nervous that she had to look at him, barely raising her lashes to view him covertly.

His eyes were on the road; she saw only the rugged lines of his profile. And something in her seemed to hurt. If only he were just a man. If only she could reach out and touch, and not be afraid . . . She closed her eyes completely, and found that she was praying again.

Don't let it be him. Please don't let it be him.

Depression suddenly weighed down heavily upon her. Would she ever know? Her luck was doomed to run out eventually. Flynn, Ian, Joshua. One of them was a crook. And they were all just charming. But one of them . . . one of them had to be a wolf in sheep's clothing.

Flynn touched her hand and she started, staring at him with wide eyes. "We're home," he said softly.

"Oh!"

"You dozed," he told her. His smile was crooked; it seemed warm now, and real.

He helped her from the car, and held a hand around her waist as they walked to the house.

Once inside, he pulled her against him; his lips hovered over the top of her head.

"Sleep tight," he said, and then he gave her a little shove toward her door. The night was over.

CHAPTER FIVE

The air was misty, soft, as if clouds had come down to earth. The sun was setting and that mist seemed to be touched by the crimson of that dying sun, making the mist pink and magical.

Brittany lay upon the sand. She could hear the ocean, the waves rolling in. She could feel the breeze, and it caressed her like a cool and gentle hand.

She could see him, coming from the mist, from the ocean. Walking smoothly, steadily, toward her. He wore that smile, that secret, knowing smile that only lovers share. He was coming toward her. In seconds, he would be with her. Bronze-tanned and hard, his eyes totally arresting, his only interest . . . her.

He smiled, and reached out a hand to her, and came down by her. His fingers laced with hers and she lay back in the sand, staring up into his eyes, completely happy though her heart skipped and vaulted and whereas the mist had been cool, his touch was fire. He would kiss her, and take her in his arms, and she wouldn't be afraid, and there would be no question that it was right. Doubts and logic had faded into the mist. All that mattered was the instinct, the instinct that he should be loved, that he could be loved, that he was as fascinated by her as she was by him—by his scent, the pulse at the base of his throat, the husky tenor of his voice, when he spoke, when he whispered love words to her.

His lips touched hers; his arms wrapped around her and she felt the hardness of his chest against the softness of her breasts and just that feeling was so erotic. As erotic as the feel of his fingers against her naked flesh . . .

Somewhere, as if from a great distance, Brittany heard a phone ringing. The sound ripped through her subconscious again and again, forcing her to wakefulness just before it ceased.

Brittany stared up at the ceiling for a long time, quivering, shaking, embarrassed that a dream could be so real.

Horrified.

She dragged herself from the bed and over to the dresser where she was confronted with her own image. A gaunt face with deep dark circles beneath the eyes. She closed them, opened them again, and the same image met her. That was what one week of living the good life at Costa del Sol had done to her. She looked awful.

And she felt worse.

She turned around and walked back, thinking that maybe, just maybe, she might sleep again. But she wouldn't, of course. She would lie there and feel thoughts and emotions churn in her heart and mind. One week. It had now been one week since Flynn Colby had fished her from the water and she had really gotten nowhere at all; she had managed only to cast herself into a dark swirling pit of pure misery.

She sat up, certain that she would not sleep, and hurried into the bathroom. She washed her face with clear cold water and felt more awake if not any less miserable.

The water was good. She took a cool shower and felt even a bit better, but when she surveyed her features in the mirror

95

again, she was still met by the pale girl with the enormous green eyes.

"You are falling in love with him—oh, you idiot!" she charged herself softly, and she wanted to deny the words, but knew that she could not. And she was frightened, frightened of the feelings, frightened of him.

There was no tangible reason for that. Flynn was always cordial, always charming. So safe. He had taken off three days —from whatever his endeavors were—to spend with her. He hadn't quizzed her, he hadn't made her uneasy. They had gone sailing, they had gone to lunch, they had toured some of the old cathedrals. He had bought her flowers, taken her to dinner, for moonlit walks on the beach.

And he hadn't touched her. Hadn't touched her at all, except to take her arm, to lead her, to set a hand upon her shoulder. To lace his fingers with hers.

Oh, God. It was just the most horrible feeling. Under normal situations, she'd be sadly pathetic to fall in love with such a man. Men like Flynn Colby didn't fall in love with women, they played with them. They entertained themselves, they went on to the next. They partied and they went yachting and they . . . made love . . .

And went on. It was a different world. Alien to anything she had ever known, and occasionally, the thought that she was here at all could send her flying into blind panic again.

And on top of it all, Flynn Colby might well be an embezzler. The thief she had come to catch. He'd lied to her; she knew that. He came and went at mysterious intervals, and he watched her like a hawk. There were a million reasons she shouldn't trust him; not one of them did a thing to change the feelings. The tension that seemed to riddle the air whenever she was near him. The longing, the aching, raw and painful, when he looked at her, when he brushed against her.

Brittany turned from the mirror, inhaling sharply and squaring her shoulders. This constant thought was going to make her go mad. The shift between panic and strength. There were times when she thought of Alice and in remembering her aunt she would feel such a rise of grief and anger at her useless death that it seemed that any move she should make, fair or foul, was necessary. Nor was she a child, she was twenty-five, she'd learned early to make her own way, make her own decisions, and stand on her own two feet. She'd known pain before; she'd lost her parents so early, and then there had been Jarod . . .

But grief had been different then. Their deaths had been acts of God, their lives had not been lost to the avarice of another.

Alice had been all that Brittany had left in the world. Her only living relative. And she had been taken so cruelly.

More the fool! Brittany thought, and she tried to tell herself that she was not falling in love with Flynn Colby, that she could take care of herself, that she would use him and anyone else in her quest to see that justice was done.

Except, she thought bleakly, that she wasn't getting anywhere. She wasn't getting anywhere at all.

She was simply falling hopelessly beneath a spell.

There was a sharp rap at her door, followed by Donald's voice.

"Ms. Martin?"

"Yes?"

Brittany hastily donned a halter dress and hurried to the door, opening it.

"Mr. Drury called earlier, Miss. I told him that you were sleeping, but he's very persistent. Can you talk now?"

"Yes, yes, thank you, Donald."

She scrambled around for a pair of sandals and hurried

down the hall behind him. The phone was set into the wall in a little niche. Brittany gave Donald an awkward smile and picked up the receiver.

"Hello, Brittany," Ian said.

"Hello, Ian."

"Lunch?"

"Pardon?"

He chuckled softly.

"Lunch, today. I've been trying to get you all week, but Flynn seems to be doing a good job of occupying all of your time."

"Oh, lunch."

She felt absurdly guilty. She needed to see Ian; she needed to force him to talk. In reality, she and Flynn were nothing to one another but she still felt guilty. Never mind that she had used the man for the entire week, she now felt like a child going behind someone's back.

She gazed around, but Donald had already disappeared.

"Brittany?"

"Lunch sounds wonderful, Ian," she murmured uncomfortably. Where was Flynn?

"I'll pick you up in half an hour then."

She hesitated only slightly. Her mouth hurt from trying to smile so frequently, and she was talking to him over the phone, but she made herself smile again anyway.

"An hour's fine, Ian."

He said something else and hung up. Brittany held the phone awhile longer, then replaced it in the cradle. She gave herself a shake and hurried back to her room, brushing her hair, applying makeup.

She hesitated then. She didn't want to see Flynn. She would blush and feel guilty all over again.

She ran downstairs and found Donald watering plants on

the terrace. As always, he gazed at her with no expression; she could never tell what Donald was thinking.

No more than she could ever really tell what Flynn was thinking. Really thinking. Sometimes when he looked at her . . .

Sometimes she could swear that he longed to hold her.

Sometimes she thought that he longed to shake her. When his eyes seemed exceptionally sharp and silver, when they seemed to slice through her, straight through her heart. Strip her naked and bare her soul.

"Donald, where is Mr. Colby, please?"

"Out for the day, Miss. He said to tell you he'll be home for dinner."

"Oh, thank you."

"Are you going out, Miss?"

"Ah, yes." She hesitated. Obviously, she had to tell Donald where she was going. "Mr. Drury is taking me to lunch."

"Yes, Miss."

Donald turned back to his plants. Maria appeared and asked Brittany if she would like coffee or breakfast and Brittany told her thank you, no, that she was going out.

It seemed forever that she waited there, with Donald silently watering plants, before the bell rang and Donald admitted Ian.

He was in a sports shirt and jeans, smiling effusively. Brittany stood when he approached; he took both her hands and gave her such a look of obvious appreciation that she flushed, uneasy.

"Thank God, I finally get a day in!" Ian laughed. He turned to Donald. "Tell your boss that she's a grown-up and I'll have her back when she's ready to come!"

"Yes, sir," Donald said simply.

Ian led her out to a little antique coupe. She didn't know

what the car was, she'd never seen one before. He set her in the passenger's seat and came around to drive, starting the car with such a roar that she jumped. He smiled, and let loose.

Ian drove fast. Very fast. She was unnerved before they had gotten anywhere at all, but he cast her a gaze with such an engaging and boyish grin that she had to smile back.

"Don't worry—I race cars sometimes."

"Oh, I'm, ah, not worried at all," Brittany lied. "Where are we going for lunch?"

His smile became a little wicked.

"My place."

"Oh."

Once they reached his house, Brittany convinced herself that she really had nothing to worry about at all. Oliver was there, Oliver was serving. He mixed them tequila sunrises which they took outside, down to the beach, where sea grapes sheltered them from the sun at a redwood patio table.

It was a beautiful setting. While they sipped their drinks Ian asked her about home, which was a good opening. If nothing else, she could describe Palm Beach to a tee, and she was easily able to talk about the exclusive shops on Worth Avenue. She even managed to twist the conversation, learning that a "chukker" in polo was merely a period of time play that could last from seven to ten minutes. If Flynn asked her questions now, she might have a few decent answers.

"I've talked about myself," Brittany told Ian ruefully. "I'd love to hear more about you."

He sipped his drink, smiling at her affectionately and she decided that she could congratulate herself, she was doing all right with Ian. She was managing to be charming—and safe.

But she couldn't really manage that with Flynn, she reminded herself. She was always afraid that if he touched her, she would forget everything. As she had when he had kissed

100

her that one time, a kiss that had led her to ridiculous dreams in which his touch followed his kiss, in which they didn't stop until . . .

"I import and export goods," he told her. "It's a nice life."

She smiled, plucking a grape from a bowl on the table. "Between Spain and England? So you travel frequently."

"All the time. I was just in England, a few weeks ago."

Her heart began to thump. He spoke so innocently.

When Flynn had lied to her.

He began to talk about his business. About his passion for cars, and for horses. She listened, she made the right comments. She felt a little ill, and then a little bit lost again, because she was wondering what she was after. No one was going to admit to her that he made his fortune by embezzling little old ladies.

Oliver served lunch, oysters on the half shell and seafood thermidor. It was delicious and she was ravenous. Brittany tried to steer the conversation toward Joshua Jones; all that she managed to learn, however, was that Joshua gambled heavily in investments and that his cash flow was often at a standstill.

"That girl of his is a problem," Ian told her.

Brittany arched a brow, wondering if Ian knew that Elly was desperately in love with him.

Apparently, he didn't. He went on to tell her that Elly was a spoiled brat, continually making her parents crazy.

"But let's forget Josh and brood, shall we?" Ian said. He stood, reaching for her hand. "Let's take a walk on the beach. Just leave your sandals. The surf feels wonderful."

A little uneasily, she took his hand. When she stood, she felt the impact of the tequila, and wished she hadn't imbibed quite so freely. She wanted to refuse him; she didn't quite dare, because if he gave up on her, she wouldn't be invited back and then she would never be able to watch him.

Depression weighed on her as she followed him along the sand. It all seemed more oblique now than ever. She was here; that much had been easy. She was managing to play the debutante all right, but where was she getting? Nowhere.

She was simply managing to fall in love with the wrong man after so many years of not feeling at all . . .

Ian had her hand. She was barely aware of the way that he was looking at her until he spoke. "So, what's it between you and Flynn? Nothing serious, I hope?"

"I beg your pardon?"

"You and Flynn. Is there anything between you?"

"He's been very kind."

Ian laughed shortly. "Surely, Brittany, you're not that naïve. I can't think of a man in the world who wouldn't be—kind—to you."

She stared out at the sea. "He's offered me hospitality, nothing more."

Ian tightened his grip around her fingers. "Then I have a chance, here, eh?"

"What?"

She stared at him. He kept smiling, but dragged her down to sit in the sand. Before she could react his fingers brushed over her cheeks and his lips pressed to hers.

He was strong. A very strong man. She fought his hold, gasping, tearing away from him.

And staring at him again, she saw that he was watchful, wary as he gazed at her.

"Ian, please—"

"I thought that I had a chance."

"I—I can't move this quickly!" she pleaded a little lamely.

Good Lord! Did rich people just roll around that easily? She couldn't believe that money could control everyone's morals!

He touched her cheek. Gently. Smiled.

"Can't blame a guy for trying, eh?" he said softly. He turned to watch the surf. "Water is beautiful, isn't it?"

Brittany inhaled and exhaled slowly, shivering with relief. She stared out at the water with him, more than willing to be sweet and companionable with the danger passed.

And totally unaware that there was a greater danger at hand.

He saw them from the house, from the glass windows overlooking the rise that led down to the beach. Saw Ian holding her hand, saw him take her into his arms.

Saw the kiss.

Saw them settle down together, a couple then, shoulders touching, friends, staring out to sea.

It was as if a million tiny firecrackers exploded within his mind; he saw red and black and red again, and felt his body burn and twist as if heated shackles of iron had been cast around him.

His fingers clenched and unclenched, and he forced himself to breathe deeply because the urge was strong, primitively strong, to run down to the beach, wrench her to her feet—and throw her over his shoulder to carry her away.

Lord . . .

All week he had known that she was just lying, that everything about her was a lie. He used the greatest restraint just to keep silent, to keep watching her. He'd been with her, touched her, laughed with her, and fought the bitter twist of emotions that arose in him every time. She was a Circe, beautiful with that auburn hair, exquisite with those emerald eyes. He'd sat there nights when he'd thought that he would erupt

103

with the longing, the raw desire to cast away her clothing and bear her down . . . anywhere . . . to have her. He'd listened to her voice, he'd heard it tremble, he'd seen the innocence in her smile.

And yet he'd known that there was no innocence. That it was some game, some ploy, that she had come with a purpose. To take him? To take someone else.

Restraint . . .

He'd held it all back. He'd been so careful. And now he felt like an inferno. Combustible. As if he couldn't trust himself to walk down to the beach. To talk, to bring her back . . .

He couldn't take his eyes off her. The flame of her hair cascading down her back. Her feet, bare and touching the water. The length of her.

He ached, he hurt, he shook. His week had been filled with fantasy. He had searched his mind and soul in fantasy, clearing her every time, making her beautiful and innocent again. He thought logically that no man could be so great a fool as to fall when he knew . . . knew that she lied.

But fantasy had remained. At work, at rest, alone, knowing that she was just feet away. He had dreamed, he had imagined. Touching her. Her throat. Following the curve of his hand with his eyes as he drew that touch lower to her breast. Down her belly to her hip. Knowing the curve, the fullness, the angles . . .

"Would you like a drink, sir?"

"What? Oh, yes, Oliver, I bloody well would."

"Ms. Martin and Mr. Drury were having sunrises. Would you prefer a Scotch?"

"Yes, Oliver, I'd prefer Scotch. Thanks. I'll take it with me."

While Oliver went for his drink, Flynn cast off his shoes and rolled up his jeans. As soon as Oliver handed him a rock glass of Scotch, he exited the back and walked along the beach to reach them.

Ian saw him first. They had been back on the subject of polo and Brittany had been listening intently. He gazed over her shoulder as he spoke, and he suddenly interrupted himself, saying, "Damn!"

"What?"

Brittany turned. It was Flynn. Feet and ankles bare and he slowly sauntered toward them. He smiled as he reached them. The sun was directly over his head, though, causing Brittany to squint to see him. And causing his eyes to seem very silver, narrow, and glittering.

"Hello," he said simply, sliding down beside Brittany. It was a hot day; he seemed to radiate heat. But his smile was so slow and lazy, Brittany thought that it had to be the sun.

"Flynn," Ian acknowledged tonelessly.

Flynn's white teeth flashed brightly against the bronze of his features. "How was lunch?"

"Delicious," Brittany murmured.

"I don't mean to be rude, old fellow, but what in God's name are you doing here?"

Flynn laughed. "I just came over to see about the game. We're supposed to be up for a charity special a week from Saturday, you do recall. Inside. Rosy, you and me against the Aussies."

"Fine," Ian agreed. "Go on then, run home now."

Again, Flynn laughed. Completely at ease, completely comfortable. "Can't leave without Brit, here. Maria insists. Seems she planned some special dinner and simply must have Brittany home tonight."

Ian was frowning. Brittany felt like protesting simply because he was acting like an elderly brother. As if he was certain that she couldn't possibly take care of herself.

She had no chance to do anything, verbally or otherwise. Flynn uncoiled himself and stood, dragging her with him. "You'll have to call back, Ian."

"Brittany," Ian scrambled to his feet, too. "Tell the Loch Ness Monster here to go home alone."

"Maria will be horribly disappointed," Flynn reminded her.

"Oh, good God," Ian moaned. "Brittany—watch out for him. And tell Maria that next Friday night she mustn't plan on you coming back for dinner. Breakfast, perhaps, but not dinner. In fact, perhaps I shall be able to persuade you not to return at all."

He gazed at Flynn and slowly, elegantly kissed her hand. Then he stepped on past them.

"That was atrociously rude!" Brittany told Flynn.

"Was it?" he queried softly. He gripped her arm. She felt that grip like a jolt of steel. "Let's go. Up the bluff—my car's in front."

"Well, my shoes aren't," Brittany said, starting back toward Ian's.

"Leave your bloody shoes," Flynn told her, and then, right then, she knew that something was horribly, horribly wrong.

"Flynn—"

"Now, Ms. Martin."

She was suddenly so frightened she felt like screaming, yet that scream died in her throat when she felt his gaze. It was all there, all the danger that hovered but never surfaced, like the tension that riddled the air but could never be touched.

Flynn's mask was down. His face was hard, his eyes were like steel and even as she struggled to determine what could

106

have come about so suddenly, he turned, dragging her up, along the bluff.

"Flynn—!"

Panting, she tried to wrench from his grasp. She stepped on a burr with her bare foot and staggered, crying out with pain. It took him several seconds to pause, and then it was only to scoop her into his arms, and carry her more quickly to his car, parked out in the long drive.

She was frightened, a little dazed from the tequila, and massively confused, though even then logic told her that she should have been forewarned. He was so hot, so tense, as if some leashed anger had suddenly been set free, and that anger was directed against her.

"Flynn . . ." It came out as a whisper. She had little choice but to lock her arms around his neck, and though she should be furious in return, she could not be righteously so, for she knew the lie she was living. Nor even as she shivered could she fight the dizzying draw, the feel of his arms about her, the hardness of his chest.

She had dreamed of his arms. Dreamed about his body. Running her fingers over the muscles in his shoulders, down his back, through his hair . . .

His heat, his touch, were suddenly gone. She had been neatly deposited in the passenger's seat of his car. The door slammed on her before she could think of bolting.

Her teeth were chattering by the time he came behind the wheel and she didn't think to speak as the ignition roared to life and the car soared like a jet out of Ian's long drive.

"Flynn—"

Face set and grim, he stared ahead at the road, giving her no heed. She sat back, gripping the door, wondering what he knew, desperately trying to think of something to say to save herself.

107

Save herself . . . she thought a bit hysterically. From what? Surely, even if he was an embezzler, he wouldn't think to—to hurt her.

No! instinct wailed again. He would never hurt her. He would never hurt her. He would never . . .

The car suddenly jerked off the main road, seeming to shriek in protest. Brittany swallowed, sinking further into her seat, then feeling a growth of anger herself. Needed anger; she wouldn't sit there cowering no matter what she had done herself, she determined fiercely.

Trees rushed by them; the car went over a dozen bumps, and then they were facing the ocean again.

On a private, lonely beach. A stretch of cool white sand completely guarded and shaded by the trees, with only the blue of the sea as witness to anything that occurred there.

Oh, God, Brittany thought, courage fading. She didn't really know the angry man sitting beside her, she didn't know him at all, only the polite and unerringly cordial mask that the stranger had chosen to show her.

Flynn sat there for the longest time, staring out at the sea. Then he opened the car door and got out. Brittany looked after him. He walked to the shore, hands in jean pockets, still barefoot, stiff, cold, unyielding. She pressed her hands against her cheeks.

God in Heaven, what did he know?

Time ticked away. She watched it disappear on the dashboard clock. And then she couldn't stand it any longer. She slammed her way out of the car and walked down to the shore where the waves washed over his feet. She kept her distance from him, at least ten feet. She placed her hands on her hips in a show of bravado and tried desperately to keep her voice from shaking.

"What? What?" It didn't work. The last rose in a scream.

And drew reaction. He turned to her, eyes blazing. They were the color of the sea, and the night. Silver blue and gray all in one, startling against his tan. And step by slow step he approached her, while she could not find the good sense to move.

"What? Ms. Martin?" he began softly. "Poor, dear Ms. Martin. Trying so hard to contact your parents. You might have mentioned that they were dead. I could have called in a medium and we could have tried a séance."

She felt as if he had struck her. She stepped back at last. "Don't," she whispered.

Oh, God, it hurt. It hadn't felt like such a terrible lie until he spoke it—his way.

He paused, cocking his head. "Why not? You apparently don't mind."

"How long—" She paused, biting her lip.

"How long have I known? Awhile now. It didn't take a great detective to discover who you were, and from there . . ." He shrugged. She noted vaguely that he had begun to walk again. That he was almost on top of her. Towering over her in anger. Suddenly all she heard was the crashing of the waves. The roar of the surf.

And then she heard his voice again. Deep, biting, cruel.

"I knew you were living a lie, Brittany. And that didn't really bother me. It intrigued me. I could never quite decide whether you were the grand impostor or a hopeless innocent. You were using me for something. And not even that bothered me. I've met fortune hunters before. It's all a game. Sometimes you win, and sometimes you lose. What finally bothered me was the realization that I just don't move fast enough for you. I wasn't enough. You had to play for Drury at the same time."

"I wasn't—"

"I saw you!"

"You saw nothing!"

It was wrong. Whatever she might have done then, what she did do was wrong. He began to laugh, and it was deep and throaty and both sexual and dangerous and even as she attempted to analyze the sound it was too late because his arms were around her and the breath was knocked from her. Suddenly she was lying in the surf and the warm ocean water was playing over her toes. Oddly, she noted the water when all the heat and warmth of his body was over hers, crushing her against the sand. She gasped and gazed upward and saw his eyes and then didn't see them at all because his head had bent low over hers, because his lips were pressed hard against hers, firm and forceful, and the edge of his tongue seared over her lips, seeking entrance.

She fought him. She clamped her lips tightly shut and pressed against the force of his chest. It was hard and unyielding. His arms felt like corded steel and her touch against them did nothing either and of all things she thought stubbornly that this shouldn't be, that she should be able to move . . .

Then he moved, of his own accord. Once again the fire of his eyes was above her, searing into her, and she thought desperately that she needed an explanation, but words had deserted her entirely.

She didn't need words. He had enough for the two of them.

"I'm so sorry, Brit. And such a fool. I stayed so near and just dreamed. Dreamed and ached—and sent you straight to Ian. Against whom you can take care of yourself. Well, here we are. Ian is a fairly hearty bloke. You can't seem to budge me, can you? Or does it even matter to you? Me or Ian—we're both rich. Is that all that you were after."

"No!" Brittany cried out in horror.

He laughed again and kissed her. A kiss that was demand-

110

ing and brutal and despite herself, she let out a sound of desperation. A cry, from deep in her throat. A protest against the force, against the brutality.

And where all her strength could not stop him, the cry did.

He did not move, his assault ceased. She felt him, the warmth, the strength, so hard against her. She felt the rasp of his breath, the pounding of his heart.

And she felt his hand against her cheek. The touch of his thumb so very gentle.

His lips touched hers. Gentle again. The tip of his tongue healed where he had been so brutal.

She touched his cheeks, instinctively. She felt all the planes there, she explored the curves and hollows. Her fingers moved into his hair and she couldn't remember his words, all she knew was the sudden sensation.

This had been her dream—the sand, the sea, the touch of the breeze . . . him. Flynn. Coming to her. Needing her. Wanting her. Instinct had told her time and again that he had to be good, that he had to be right.

She couldn't remember why she was there, how she had come to the Costa del Sol, how and why she had come to this place. She was mesmerized by sensation. The feel of his breath against her flesh. The tip of his tongue, first against her lips, then gaining entrance beyond, finding the most insinuative and erotic pleasure there.

The feelings were good, and deliciously right. More feelings. His fingers at the nape of her neck, finding the hook to the halter dress. Breaking it apart, pulling the material down and baring her breasts to the sun and the breeze . . .

And his gaze.

"My God."

He murmured things against her throat. Against a pulse that thundered there, against the lobe of her ear, against her breast before he took the taut nipple into his mouth, laving it again and again. Her fingers locked into his hair. She felt a great rumbling within her. A trembling, hot and fluid. Where he touched her, the feeling was fire. Where he did not touch her, the warmth spread anyway. She had never felt so totally weak.

So desperate to know more.

Perhaps it was the tequila. Perhaps it was the breeze, or the sound of the sea, a heartbeat that joined with her own. She didn't think to protest. She didn't want to protest. She didn't want anything to come between them, to come between what was, and what could be.

She didn't know if there really was a pink haze, a crimson mist of sunset. She just knew that it was a dream. That it had begun the first time she had seen him, that it had been growing ever since. Each time she inhaled his scent. Each time she felt his eyes or the brush of his fingers against her.

He stared at her, and she returned that stare. Her lips grew dry as she fought for air. She touched them at last with her tongue and brought movement from him again. His hand, searching along her thigh, traveling higher and higher, bringing the skirt of her dress with it. She moaned softly at the touch of his fingers, inhaling sharply, so dizzy with the sharpness of sensation that she would have fallen were she not already down. She felt weak; she felt alive. There must be . . . more. That she ached for something intangible that had to come . . .

He said something, he muttered something. The little strip of lace broke and she was aware that she was bare above the waist and below and he was looking at her and that she should have been embarrassed or horrified and she was neither; she was only anxious, unable to move, praying that he didn't go away.

Another hoarse sound escaped him and he was on his knees above her, casting away his shirt, unzipping his jeans. She did not draw her eyes away, but watched him, too.

And more warmth sizzled through her. Warmth created by the fine breadth of his shoulders, by their bronze glow. By the deep brush of dark hair upon his chest, tapering at his waist, to grow in profusion again below, to nest and cloak . . .

The urgency of his sex.

He gave off a husky little cry. She felt his arms around her; the delicious stroke of his tongue within her mouth. She gave way to temptation. Her fingers pulsed and caressed along his nape, along the length of his spine. She felt him, so much a part of her already. All that she breathed, the fire, the trembling, the hard, rampant thunder of his heart . . .

His hand, stroking her thigh, then his weight, settling over her, between her.

Her breath caught with sudden pain. She would have cried; she bit into her lips instead. Her nails curved against him with no conscious volition, yet when he would draw away she twisted her head and held to him fast.

He whispered things to her. She opened her eyes and the sun was setting. The air around them was in rainbow shades; the surf continued to pound as if it were inside of her.

She bit lightly against his shoulder. She was seared, as if electricity flowed through her.

She could not let him go.

He moved.

Slowly . . . quickly. And the feeling rose. Rose like lightning, rose like thunder, rose like the most wondrous storm, tense and exciting, vivid, exquisite. The moments were so keen, so precious. She wanted it to go on forever. She ached so, she reached so, it was a bit like dying.

Like dying . . .

It was life. Life so keen, so acute, it was painful.

Life . . .

She reached for a star, and plucked it from the heavens. She shivered, she arched, she shuddered, and yet that was not all, but again and again in little aftershocks.

She opened her eyes. She saw his face. Tense, taut, strained. He cast his back and moved against her again and she felt him shudder, shudder, tremble . . . as she had. Shudder, and fill her, and fall against her, and they were both damp and panting and exhausted beneath the sun.

Slowly, slowly, the glow faded from her. The breeze touched her and she was cool, and then acutely aware of what she had just done.

And she was still speechless.

Flynn moved away from her at last. She closed her eyes and swallowed miserably.

She felt rather than saw that he adjusted his jeans and zipped them, and walked back, ankle deep, to stare into the water.

Self-consciously, she smoothed her skirt down. She drew the bodice against herself and fumbled to fix the strap, then realized that it was broken.

He turned then to stare at her.

Face dark, intent, brooding. Somehow bewildered, somehow furious . . .

"All right," he said. His voice and his expression seemed to mask a thousand things, "I'll marry you."

She stared at him, incredulous, then furious.

Close to tears.

She had dreamed of him; she hadn't dared to dream those words. Yet spoken, they seemed the most horrible insult she had ever heard.

She gasped, and stood, somehow holding her dress before her, somehow clinging to dignity.

"Don't be absurd! Don't be—archaic! I wouldn't marry you if—I would *never* marry you!" she hurled at him.

And then she spun, hurrying for the car, hurrying lest her tears should fall and he should see them.

He caught her arm and spun her around. "Wasn't that the grand plan?" he demanded harshly.

"What?" she demanded, outraged and amazed.

He laughed dryly.

"The siren from the sea, Ms. Martin. A sweet young innocent seduced and deflowered, or whatever the bloody hell the term is these days."

She just stared at him, and then she began to laugh hysterically.

He really didn't know a damn thing about her.

Just her name. And her income.

And oh, God, she hurt so badly, so badly, and she couldn't let him know . . .

"Go to hell, Mr. Colby," she said flatly. And she shook off his arm and started walking down the beach.

The pity was, she had nowhere to go.

She was too upset to know it.

CHAPTER SIX

"Brittany!"

She knew that he was coming after her. She felt the pounding of his feet against the sand. A combination of misery and stupidity sent her racing into the surf.

He was behind her.

"Brittany!"

His arms came around her, strong arms, tight arms, arms that were attempting to subdue. But she was in her element now. Water. Water all around her. The clean, azure sea, with the bottom far, far below.

She jackknifed her legs with a powerful thrust, going downward, eluding even his grasp. She felt his hands, grasping for her. Another swift kick sent her spiraling away.

His hand caught the fabric of her flimsy gown. He kept the fabric but he lost her.

It was insane; she kept swimming anyway. Yet for all her prowess, he was strong enough to keep up with her. He caught her again and again. Hands against her bare flesh. Again and again she eluded him, not hearing his shouts, heedless of anything except the will to be alone, away, somewhere far from him to think upon the total folly of her actions.

Of the pain.

"Brittany, damn it!"

His hands, hot and warm against the water, came upon her. Coursed along her body, slick and grasping, as she jackknifed again.

She wanted to be alone. To lick her wounds.

In the end, she simply tired. He caught her, and she simply hadn't the strength left to vault away again. His arm came around her waist and he dragged her back to the shore, placing her there, reclining beside her, that arm still warily across her middle lest she should think to flee again.

He was panting heavily. Dripping wet and panting heavily and leaning over her. She closed her eyes. She tried not to think that she was caught. That he had known a certain truth all along. That he had been playing with her as a cat might right before the kill.

That she had just made love with him. Because she had wanted to. Foolishly, ridiculously. Against all good sense. Because she had fallen in love with one of the very men she had come to watch, to catch for a thief . . .

And her dress was somewhere out in the surf. The breeze was caressing her naked flesh and bringing painfully home to her the extent of her vulnerability.

What did he intend to do?

Nothing . . . ? He was still breathing deeply. Still hovering over her. She didn't open her eyes. She felt the warmth of his breath where it touched her cheeks, her throat. She felt his arm, a bar across her waist. She felt the drenched material of his jeans, for his knee was cast lightly over her thighs, another bar of the prison he created with his body.

She was so cold. The sun was setting, yet the air was warm. She started to shiver, acutely aware of the misery of her position. Cold and wet and of course her nipples were hardening and she was so totally humiliated that she discovered it was possible to want to die from the horror of the feeling.

117

"Brittany . . ."

It was sound, it was warning, it was a question she couldn't begin to answer.

"Just—just let me go," she finally managed to whisper. She still couldn't open her eyes. Couldn't face him. "Just let me go. I'll disappear, you'll never—"

"You're not going anywhere," he told her quietly. "Until I start getting some answers. Open your eyes—and talk to me."

She really didn't want to. She felt like an ostrich. If she didn't open her eyes, she didn't have to be lying here, stark naked beneath his malevolent glare.

"Brittany." It was a ragged, forceful prod.

"I—I can't. I can't talk, like this . . ."

Her eyes did open. Perhaps her pain and misery were mirrored within them for he paused. His expression didn't alter one bit from harshness, but he moved away from her. He rose with a natural athletic grace, found his knit shirt in the sand, and brought it back to her. She lowered her eyes, silently grateful, and scrambled into the shirt. It was huge on her and fell to her thighs.

He didn't give her much time. He sat down beside her. She inhaled sharply, aware that he was so close that he actually sat on the tail of the shirt.

A guarantee that she would not bolt again?

She realized the futility of an escape attempt and she felt like sobbing. The road was at least a mile back and she couldn't begin to imagine herself nude and peso-less on an open highway.

"Talk to me, Brittany."

She stared ahead of her, out to the azure waters. She ground her teeth together and thought of what a fool she was. Proof that grief could indeed lead to insanity. She was in over her head. Oh, so far over . . .

He'd known from the very beginning.

She shook her head, suddenly, bitterly.

"There's nothing to say. You were right before. I was after your money. I showed up in Costa del Sol to catch your eye." She cast a glance in his direction, smiling with no humor. "I really don't think you're worth it after all. Thanks, but no thanks. So if you'll just drive me back——"

Her voice died along with her smile. He didn't blink, he just stared at her, ruthless, cold, totally hard.

"You're not who you say you are," he began. "And I've changed my mind—you're definitely not after my money." She was silent. He continued.

"I'll start for you, shall I? Your parents were killed ten years ago. Together—they were drowned in a canal."

"The windows," Brittany heard herself murmur.

"What?"

"The—the car went off the road into a canal. Mother always hated electrical windows. They didn't work. By the time the pressure equalized, the doors locked in the muck at the bottom."

She didn't look at him, she stared down at the sand. A little crab was burrowing into a hole. She longed to be doing the same. She hadn't caught a thief. She'd merely . . . lost her soul.

He was silent for a moment, as if swayed by sympathy for the briefest moment.

"You lived with the Ericsons. Majored in Marine Science at Florida State. You work for the State on Cocoa Beach. Two months ago you took an extended leave of absence and appeared in London—for a funeral. Then you appeared on a plank in the sea. Why?"

"I told you——"

"Why?"

"I don't have——"

"You owe me an explanation."

"The hell I do——"

"The hell you don't, lady."

She started to rise in the sand. He caught her elbow and brought her back down, hard.

She started to shiver, hot and then cold. She had decided deep in her heart that it could not be this man. This man who had entered her dreams and then her flesh. And she would never pretend, not even to herself. She had wanted him so desperately. The fantasy had been an irresistible allure, and the reality . . .

Had been more than she could ever imagine.

Just as the stark pain and horror now. She couldn't tell him the truth.

What if she was wrong?

What if he was a crook, oh, God, she had to remember that he had lied to her, but, oh, God, that hadn't mattered just minutes ago, she had believed in her heart . . .

"I've got all night," he warned her.

She gazed to him sharply, suddenly furious. "Well, I don't. If you would please——"

"Outrage, indignation. Wonderful. You came to me with all false pretenses, and you're angry. Sorry. We're sitting here until you decide you want to tell me what's going on."

"Why should I tell you? You've already decided."

"Ah, yes, but you turned down my offer. So let's have the truth."

"What difference does it make to you?" she asked with sudden dismay.

He shifted, stretching out on the cool sand, resting upon an elbow, but continuing to watch her with no sign of compassion, no mercy—no humanity.

"Tremendous difference," he told her. "I'm waiting."

"My God, you're not human!"

He lowered his eyes and smiled at that, then met her eyes again with a trace of amusement. "All too human, I'm afraid. What the hell did you think you were doing with Ian?"

The change of direction threw her. "Ian?"

"Yes, lunch. And other things."

"There were no 'other things.' "

"Let's not go through with this. You're after something. What is it? What is it you could want so badly that you would play dangerous games with the two of us?"

"There was nothing dangerous—"

"Oh. That's right. You can handle Ian. Tell me—did you handle me?"

"God, I'm not going to listen—"

Once again, she tried to rise. Once again, she found herself back in the sand. Flat now. And he was crawling over her again and though she had his shirt it rose against her with his movement and she was bare beneath the waist and horribly aware of his hip and his thigh and the dampness of his jeans and the heat of his body beneath.

"You are going to listen. And so am I."

She closed her eyes. She breathed deeply.

"Did you handle me, Brittany?"

"No. Yes. No. I could have. I—"

"Could have?" She heard the depth of his voice. The husky burr. It came against her with greater power than anything physical could have done.

She shook her head, denying herself, denying him.

"Could have," he repeated softly. He brushed a finger over her cheek, following the movement with his eyes. Then he smoothed damp red hair from her forehead and watched that movement, too.

"You're very good in the water," he said suddenly. "You've been a lifeguard?"

"Yes."

"Breaking holds . . . you assumed you could break any of Ian's holds if things got out of hand?"

"Yes."

"You know there is only so far you can push any man?"

She didn't really understand the question. Nor the touch of his eyes. Silver, hooded.

"Please, let me go."

"No," he said simply. "You say that you could have handled me—but you didn't. I'm not so sure that I believe the first, yet I'm dying to hear you expand upon the second. Let's see. You're after something, and you want it so badly that you were willing to make love with me to get it—"

"No!"

"But you did." His eyes glittered dangerously. "Just what *are* you after?"

"Oh, God, please—"

"Brittany, all we need here is a little truth. A lot of it actually, but we'll start off with a little. Why?"

"Why what?" she nearly screeched.

"Why did you sleep with me?"

"Because I wanted to!" She screamed it out and furiously tried to escape him. He didn't budge. The slightest smile twitched against the corners of his mouth.

"Is that the truth?"

"Yes. For the love of God—"

"We're just beginning to get places. I'll go back and refresh your memory again. You were in London. For a funeral. An elderly aunt of yours passed away. You claimed to have been accosted by El Drago. Is that the truth?"

"I—"

"The truth."

"No. Dammit, please—"

"So sorry. Let's go onward here. You needed to become part of the social fabric of the Costa del Sol British community. Why?"

She stared at him, at the unrelenting planes of his face, at the sharp, hard, bronzed angles there. She became aware of his fingers, entwined with her own.

She closed her eyes suddenly, shivering miserably. She knew so little about him. She knew his face, she knew the nuances of his smile. She knew that day by day she had come to love the rugged beauty of his face, the magic of his scent, the cadence of his voice. Little by little, day by day.

And now . . .

Now while he demanded and threatened, she loved the feel of his fingers against hers. She loved him simply there, hard against her, and somehow secure.

She inhaled and exhaled, looking at him searchingly. Praying that she was right. That she was not a fool.

"I had to catch a thief," she said softly.

He frowned. "What?"

And she didn't dare look at him then, she had made her decision and there really wasn't anything else to do. She closed her eyes and felt the sea through the sand and tried to explain what had happened and how she had felt and how very desperate she had been.

"My aunt Alice was my last living relative. I adored her. When my parents died, she was all that I had. And she was healthy and spry and wonderful and she never would have died except that—she was taken. I learned from the neighbors that she was terribly enthused about a young man helping her with her investments. She gave him everything. Her life's savings. And when he came for the final capital, something

123

must have warned her. She tried to catch him. She was too old to run down the streets . . . she had a heart attack and died."

"I'm sorry," Flynn said softly. "But I don't understand. How did that bring you here?"

She looked at him, wry, sad, only slightly bitter. "There have been a number of such cases. The police know that a British citizen has been ripping off dozens of elderly people in and around London. They were able to tell me that they were certain that their man was basing himself at Costa del Sol. English is so freely spoken—and there is no extradition agreement. It's someone who lives very well, someone cultured, someone rich. I checked the airlines schedules and came up with a list of names of suspects—wealthy Britons living here who were in England at the time. Men with questionable means—"

"And I was number one on your list?"

She shook her head.

"It didn't matter where you were on my list. I learned about El Drago through the papers—and I learned where you would be. It—it seemed simple enough, and then it seemed ridiculous and horrible and stupid—but by then, I was already in your house."

"You came down here with nothing, you threw yourself into the sea on a plank—to catch a thief?"

"A murderer!" Brittany cried out defensively. "Don't you see? He killed her!"

He looked away from her, rose slowly, and walked out in the surf. It was growing darker. The whole shoreline was a dusky hue. Beautiful, barren, lonely.

He spun back around to her. "You idiot! Didn't it ever occur to you that this man could be dangerous? What were you expecting to do? Walk up and ask us all if we had embezzled your aunt's savings? Then what? Drag the guilty one to a British Airways flight home and have the police waiting?"

"No! No!" Brittany cried out hoarsely. "I knew what I was doing—"

"Bloody hell, you did!"

Brittany stood, knotting her fingers nervously into fists at her side. "I was going to get to know you all—and talk about money. Money to be invested. Only I'd have to go back to England to get it and once I went for the money, I could have told Brice what I'd done and he could have—"

"Brice?"

"A friend of mine with the police in London."

"Oh. Tell me, does this Brice person know that you're here?"

She shook her head.

"Little fool."

"Dammit! What the hell was I supposed to do? Let this man get away with murder?"

He looked at her for a long while.

"You're going to go home," he said softly.

"What? I—I can't! I've come this far, don't you understand, I can't just let it go!"

"I'm getting you on the next plane out."

She raised her head to him furiously. "Why? Have I been wrong? Are you the one I should be after?"

He grinned at her. "You were after me and you got me. Rather well, actually."

Brittany stared at him, then swung around, shoulders straight as she headed for the car. He followed her, settling into the driver's seat even as she slammed her door. She tried to ignore the fact that she was wearing his shirt and he was wearing his jeans with his chest bare. She tried not to look at him.

She tried very hard not to burst into tears, and stared straight ahead through the window.

"I'm not leaving Costa del Sol. Of course, I've no intention of accepting any more of your hospitality—"

Flynn reached into the glove compartment for a pack of cigarettes. He slowly lit one, inhaled and exhaled, leaning back in the driver's seat not yet ready to start the car.

"Where do you think you'll go?"

"If I'm to believe that you're innocent, then I've only two suspects left. I'll—"

"Who?"

"It's not your—"

"Who?"

"Ian and Joshua."

"So you'll just go stay with one of them."

Brittany sat silently, staring at her hands.

He inhaled again, then rested his hands idly against the steering wheel.

"No, you won't," he said at last.

"I can't stay with you. Not after today."

"You should be on your way home. I understand—"

"You don't understand anything!"

"Be that as it may. Forget about going to Drury's."

"I—"

"Forget it. Entirely. Now. If you were to do something like that, I'd feel obliged to warn him that you were after his throat."

"He may not care," Brittany challenged sweetly, but he gave her such a withering glare that she was quickly sorry that she had spoken.

"You don't mind paying for hospitality, eh?"

She reached in a sudden blind motion for the door; he

126

reached over and caught her hand with his, and then her eyes with his own.

"I'm sorry. Brittany, I'm sorry. I just can't let you go to Ian's. You can't do it. If you've absolved me of guilt, then you know yourself that it must be Ian or Josh—if your information is right. You can't go to Ian's."

She looked down at his hand on her own.

"I can't stay with you after today."

"Why not?"

"Because . . ."

He caught her chin, tilting her face toward his. Darkness was coming swiftly now. In the dimming light, mauve and gray, she saw a subtle spark in his eyes and the tenderness that had been missing before.

"I thought you said that we made love because you wanted it to happen."

"I did," she whispered in return. "But I can't go back with you now. I'd be . . ."

"Kept?" He laughed.

She flushed. "I don't know exactly what I mean or what I feel, only that I—I don't know what to do."

"Go home."

"I can't. I can't forget that Alice was swindled and for all intents and purposes—murdered."

Flynn lit another cigarette, hesitated, then started the car. "Two choices, Brittany. You leave the country, or you come home with me."

She didn't answer him. He let the car idle, then he turned it off again. He reached for both of her hands and he was still smiling, the gaze was still tender, and she realized with a throbbing beat of her heart that she really had fallen in love with him, and that everything that had happened here today had compounded the feeling, dragged it deeper and deeper into her soul.

He turned the ignition again. He didn't speak, nor did she, as the car left the beach path behind and came upon the open road. Brittany felt the wind take and whip her damp hair into a wild froth that swirled about her, and the feeling was good, it was cleansing, yet it did nothing to ease the tumult in her mind. How had he known so much, when had he known, what in God's name had she done, and what on earth did she do now?

The questions, the feelings, rose and whirled inside of her as wild as the tangle of her hair.

And there were no answers to be found.

She was still lost in thought and emotion when the car came to a halt. She realized that he was staring at her. And then she realized that they were both barefoot—that she wore his shirt, and he wore his jeans.

"We'll go through the back," he said softly.

But going through the back didn't help; they still had to come upon the courtyard—and company was there.

"Ian," Flynn said, startled.

Ian Drury lifted a glass to his host. "Wonderful martini— Donald is a magnificent host in your absence, Flynn. I'd thought to catch you for coffee—following that dinner Maria was to have made. That special dinner." He smiled and indicated a little tote bag on the floor. "I was returning your shoes."

Brittany swallowed uneasily, keenly aware of her appearance. And of Ian Drury's mocking gaze upon her.

Flynn's hands came protectively to her shoulders; she felt herself pulled against the hardness of his muscled chest.

"Thanks, Ian. Where is Donald? I think I'd like a drink myself. Brittany?"

"Please," she said, and had to repeat the word because no sound came from her.

Flynn sauntered casually over to the bar. Brittany still couldn't seem to take a step or even move. While Flynn poured drinks, Ian continued to stare at her, smiling. "Ms. Martin, for a lady who likes to take things slowly, you do seem to be rather careless with your clothing. Last I remember, you were wearing a dress."

She didn't have a chance to grope for a reply. Flynn turned around with their drinks, laughing.

"Brittany, is that what you told this poor man? Ian, my boy, I am sorry. Brit and I had a tiff this morning. Otherwise, she certainly would have let you know that we've . . . well, next week we're going to look for the ring. A simple solitare, I think. Old-fashioned and perfect."

Brittany stared at him incredulously. He didn't blink; he smiled easily, laconically. He came to her, eyes sparkling savagely upon hers, to hand her a glass.

She detested Scotch. She swallowed down a massive gulp anyway.

"Really?" Ian demanded.

"Of course."

Flynn came around behind her again, slipping his free hand around her, pulling her back against himself again. "Do tell Ian that you're sorry, luv."

She bared her teeth into a smile. This was disaster. Of course, she was horribly humiliated to be caught dressed so— or undressed so, but now she would never be able to come close enough to the man to discover anything.

"Brittany." He whispered her name low and close to the lobe of her ear and little hot streaks like lightning rippled through her.

She couldn't stay here now! Not with him. Not knowing—

him. Wanting him. Losing all thought and logic and concentration because of him.

Ian Drury was still staring at her, politely awaiting an answer.

"Flynn," she said softly, apologetically returning Ian's gaze. "It really wasn't like that at all. This morning—"

"All right, I agree. We were both monstrous." He grimaced to Ian. "Lovers' quarrels. Like hell itself. But as you can see—" He paused, shrugging. "—solved now."

Ian nodded and set his glass down. "Yes. As I can see. Well, then I'll be going. My very best to the two of you. When is the happy occasion?"

"Oh, not for a long while—" Brittany began.

"Soon," Flynn said simultaneously.

"Oh," Ian said, as if their answers had not crossed at all. He smiled again. "Well, then, I'll be seeing you both soon. I do take it that dinner is off next week. Pity. Ms. Martin, you never gave me a chance. Flynn—you are a bloody hog."

"Had to be. I didn't dare let my mermaid get too far out of my sight."

Ian nodded again and waved, and strode out of the courtyard. Flynn called a pleasant good night to him.

After he left, there was utter silence on the courtyard. Flynn followed his disappearance with brooding eyes.

And then Brittany exploded.

"What on earth did you do that for?"

"Do what?" Flynn walked over to the patio table, sliding into one of the chairs, planting his feet upon another.

"That—that—engagement charade? Now I'll never get close to him!"

"Damned right you won't, my lass," Flynn said softly, studying his glass.

"Damned right? I didn't appoint you my keeper, Flynn

Colby!" Brittany followed him over to the table and stared down at him.

He moved his feet back to the floor and folded his hands over the table, meeting her gaze levelly.

"Brittany—a blind man would know what we'd been up to. You're underestimating Ian. If I hadn't staked a solid claim . . ." His voice trailed away and he laughed suddenly. "I rather thought that I was doing the gentlemanly thing. Tell me, Brittany, how do I win with you?"

Confused, she backed away from the table. Her knees hit one of the chairs and she fell into it and pressed her temple between her fingers. "Flynn, don't you see? I have to know, I have to do something; my God, why do you think that I tried that foolish ruse about El Drago to begin with?"

"Brittany, I do see," he told her softly. She didn't hear him rise, but suddenly he was before her, bending down, reaching for her hands. She saw his shoulders, broad and bronze and gleaming in the soft light, all the muscles seeming to ripple and dance. She saw his eyes and that strange tenderness was in them again and once more she experienced an acute tear of emotions. She was in love with him; she was terrified to be in love with him. She hadn't come here to fall in love . . .

And certainly not with Flynn Colby.

"Brittany, trust me. I'll help you."

"Help me?" she repeated softly.

"Yes. You won't have to go it alone. You won't have to set yourself up in dangerous situations. We'll do it together. Brittany. First, I swear to you I never knew your aunt. I've never swindled an old lady in my life. Or a young one, for that matter. I have connections, I have sources. Trust me, and I'll help you."

She nodded slowly.

And just then, Donald came walking out to the courtyard. So very, very correct in black suit.

"Oh, dear, dear, sir, I hadn't known that you'd returned. Shall you have dinner now, or—"

He stopped in midstride and midsentence, taken aback by their apparel. But then, he was Donald, so his break was a small one.

"Or shall you be changing first?"

"Oh, I think we'll change, Donald, thank you. Brittany, will forty-five minutes be enough to shower and dress?"

She nodded. And somehow—feeling as if she were bare to the bone with no secrets whatsoever—she managed to rise with a pretense at dignity, smile at Donald, and walk along with Flynn toward the elevator.

CHAPTER SEVEN

There were a million little things that changed once you were lovers, Brittany thought. Beautiful little things. Like the way you looked at one another over wineglasses. When fingers brushed, when eyes met. Knees touching beneath the table, a special new cadence to his voice, to hers, a huskiness . . .

I'm hopeless, she warned herself. But then it was true, she had known herself out of her depth since she first saw him, and after that she had begun to give up little pieces of herself, bit by bit. And naïve as it might be, she could really do nothing now but cherish the excitement and the warmth, and the belief.

There really couldn't have been any halfway point in this. She had been forced to trust him. And God help her if she was wrong.

When Donald had left them with spicy palomino steaks, Flynn poured wine and admitted he'd given her the closest thing he could find to vinegar on their first night together. Anger had welled within her but he had been laughing and suddenly she found herself laughing too. But then she sobered again, unable to forget her reason for being there.

"Flynn," she murmured, enjoying the flavor of a true vintage Riesling, "what am I going to do? You really have rather destroyed any chance that I—"

His fingers curled over hers, gripping them warmly.

"I asked you to trust me, to let me handle this."

"But it's my problem—"

"I can handle it better than you can."

"But what do I do now?"

He smiled, looking down at his plate, then back at her. "You come away with me."

"What?"

She wanted to pull her fingers back. This was the part of the situation she despised. While showering, she had mulled over everything. She had burned and sizzled with remembrance and pressed her fingers to flaming cheeks, and tried desperately to analyze it all.

If only he had been a beach bum. An employee of AT&T. Someone who she might have met casually . . .

She was twenty-five. She endured a fair amount of tragedy in those years. She'd learned to be independent, to live alone, to work and play and like it.

She deserved an affair. Some laughter, some love. Some experience. If only . . .

If only she didn't know his reputation. If only he came from a world that she understood . . . where she belonged.

"Let's go away," he repeated.

"Away? Where? Why?"

He laughed, releasing her hand. "Away from here. Somewhere private. To get to know one another."

"I—I don't think that I can," she murmured, lowering her eyes and feeling a crimson flush rise over her again.

"Why?"

"That would really make me a kept woman."

He didn't laugh, but she felt that his lips curled with a tender amusement.

"It's really not amusing—"

134

"Brittany, you're here with me, one way or another. Unless you're willing to forget the whole thing and go home."

"I can't—"

"That's right. So what difference does it make. Brittany—" He came around the table and caught her chin, raising her eyes to his. "Today, on the beach—you said that what happened was what you wanted. Only once? Aren't you willing to take a chance? To explore further, to see what else is there for us?"

"I know what's there," she told him softly, with a rueful smile. "I read all about you before I came here."

"Oh, God," he groaned. "But still, on the beach . . ."

His voice trailed away; she sought for an answer but could find none when he was so close.

She was reprieved from an explanation then because Donald interrupted.

"Mr. Colby. Telephone, sir." He hesitated. "Returning your call."

"Oh, yes, thank you, Donald."

He withdrew from her, expression changing, becoming pensive and somehow dark.

And in this case, Donald did not bring the phone to the table. Flynn excused himself saying that he wouldn't be long, and left her.

Brittany sipped more wine, trying to think of what she should say or do. She thought it over too many times. Her mind seemed to be burned out, she couldn't think at all. She just felt tired.

Tired . . .

But though she protested it, still strangely alive. Yes, oh God, yes, she wanted to explore, to be with him, to feel him, to laugh with him . . . to love him.

135

* * *

Flynn stood at the hallway phone, listening to Chief Betancourt's verifications.

"Alice Whalen, aged seventy-three, died of a heart attack on Baker Street. Apparently she was sharper than some of the others—something in their last meeting convinced her that she had been taken by a scam artist. Bloody good trick at that —we haven't a single solid description of the man."

"Do you think it's the same man we've been after?" Flynn asked his immediate superior.

"Quite possibly. You can find out."

"How?"

"He's been accepting more than cash. He's been taking jewelry. Easy to melt down and dispose of in either Spain or Morocco. Have you had any luck yet?"

"No, but I'll be making another play soon."

"What about the girl?"

"What about her?"

"What are you going to do with her?"

"Do? Why, nothing, Chief. She's my guest here. What would you have me do?"

"I'd have you be careful. What you're doing is dangerous. There's no help I can give you if you're obstructed in any way. I'd deny having ever seen your face, and you know damned well, my boy, why that has to be."

"I'm all right, Chief."

"Are you?"

"Of course."

The Chief laughed suddenly. "Bloody good ruse, bloody good damn ruse that was! El Drago having left her a pauper. You'd best watch your tail, boy."

"I will."

"Ta, then. I'll be hoping for some good news soon."

"I hope so, sir."

Flynn waited until the line from London went dead. He held the receiver for a moment and thought that the Chief was right; if he had any sense in his head whatsoever, he'd have her on the next flight out of the country.

But he couldn't send her away. She was determined. And if he let her out of his sight, it was possible that he could really cast her into danger.

But do I dare take a chance, having her so close?

Wanting her so badly . . .

Not now, you fool! He warned himself. This was not the time to fall in love . . . To let down his guard in the least, to take the slightest chance . . .

He closed his eyes and slammed a fist against the wall. I am not taking a chance! She'd lied, yes, but now he knew why, and he knew that everything that she had said today was true.

Trust no one; that was the key.

But he didn't have to tell her anything. His life and their lives—what could be—were totally separate. And right now . . .

Right now he couldn't change his course if his life depended on it. It had started when he'd pulled her from the ocean. Then he'd seen her, here, in his home, at his table. He watched her smile. He'd seen the way the sun caught and reflected and dazzled in her hair and caught all the brilliant emerald teasing lights in her eyes.

He held her away because he'd known he'd taken a siren from the sea, and he'd had the sense to take care, but all that sense had meant nothing today when he'd followed her to Ian's, when he'd seen Ian touch her. And like an irate and possessive fool he'd dragged her down to the beach but even after all his horrid behavior she'd touched him, she'd wanted him, and he'd become one with her and now . . .

It wasn't the time to fall in love.

He turned around and started back to the table. Love knew no time. He didn't intend to be stupid.

He didn't intend to let her go, either.

But when Flynn reached the table, she was gone.

"Ms. Martin left her apologies with me, sir. She has retired for the night."

Flynn arched a brow. Donald watched him challengingly, but didn't say any more.

"Thank you," Flynn said.

"Shall you have coffee?"

Flynn shook his head and then grinned at Donald, too. "I shall retire for the evening, too."

"Flynn!"

He swung back around, grinning. "Mind your position now, Donald."

"You mind your manners."

"I'm in love, Donald."

"My arse—sir—if you don't mind me sayin' so!"

He laughed softly. "Oh, you doubting Thomas! Out of my own ranks!"

Donald pursed his lips and held silent for a moment.

"It isn't a good time to be falling in love, sir."

"I told myself that very thing. But don't you worry, Donald. About either of us."

Whistling, Flynn went up to his own room.

He showered vigorously with cold water. It didn't help. He donned a robe and opened the balcony doors and looked out on the night, then he paced the floor for a while. He thought about what he was going to do. It was wrong, of course.

But he couldn't help it.

He opened the closet, slid the back panel, and found himself in the darkness in a froth of lace. Lace that all seemed to

138

carry her scent. The door to her closet was ajar. He pushed it farther and saw that she was lying in bed in something very soft and slinky, something that clung to her in the moonlight. But even in the moonlight, her hair was on fire—a sea of flame that cascaded over the pillow where she lay.

He walked over to her. She nearly screamed. She bolted upright, bringing her covers along with her.

"How—"

"The closets connect."

"You've got no right—"

"But I do, Brittany. Really," he told her huskily, sitting beside her on the bed, stroking her cheek. "I earned the right when I met a siren from the sea who cast out her tempting song and brought me crashing in upon the rocks."

"The closets connect?" she murmured skeptically, but she was smiling as he touched the thin little spaghetti strap at her shoulder and eased it down her arm to press a kiss there. His arms came around her, they eased back down to the bed. He spread her hair out over the pillow and for a long moment their eyes met. His body ached and throbbed with each breath that she took, and he thought again that it was no time to fall in love, but that he would surely die in slow painful degrees if he did not love her. Then he kissed her and she wrapped her arms around him, her fingers threading into his hair, holding him tight against her. Her tongue, liquid and darting, delicately rimmed his lips. He drew it into his mouth, plunged his own into hers and felt himself tremble with the aching awareness, yearning desire.

They broke apart and her eyes met his. He came back to her, hungry—kissed her lips again and again, her cheeks, her chin, her throat. His mouth skimmed her shoulder and with those kisses he brought down the lacy froth of the nightgown baring her breasts.

139

Her skin was lightly perfumed and the scent seemed an elixir. He drew her breast into his mouth, cradling the weight, innately aware of the instinctive curl of her body to his, the soft, sweet rasp of her breath, the touch of her hands against him.

"Night after night . . . I lay awake," he whispered, moving from her, shifting the gown. "I knew you were here. So close. And I knew you were lying and I didn't know why and I wanted what came to us not to be a lie . . . I'd have never hurt you," he told her. "Never, with malice, would I have—"

She touched his lips with her fingers and smiled. "Stop, please. Don't speak."

"You smell wonderful. You taste wonderful. If I were truly to crash against the rocks, I don't think I'd give a damn . . ."

"Flynn . . ."

She touched his forehead, smoothing his hair. Her eyes were wide and clear and he shuddered, touched by the soft awe in them, by the evocative combination of sophistication and pure innocence that made her so unique. That made it more than . . .

Wanting.

"Touch me," he whispered hoarsely to her, and she did. The palm of her hand rubbed against his chest, her fingers threading lightly through the mass of short hair there, slipping beneath the V of his robe, playing tentatively with muscles and flesh. Then more boldly, and slipping lower and lower. She found the belt and untied it and he haphazardly tossed his robe aside and he caught her gown and eased it from her and then . . .

He could wait. Wait to stare at her in the moonlight, the beautiful curves and angles of her body. His heart hammered and he couldn't move.

She made a little sound, reaching for him, and he caught her hand, shaking his head slightly. "Brittany . . ."

He'd seen her in a skimpy bikini. He'd made love to her already. But he'd never seen her like this . . .

"Flynn." She slipped her arms around his neck and pulled him back to her, nipping at his throat, his shoulders, touching her lips to his again and again.

"I'm just not . . . very good at . . . I'm not . . ."

He laughed and caught her cheeks tenderly between his palms and told her earnestly, "Brittany, no one can learn what you create. What you give. What you do to me."

She sighed softly and kissed him again. He slid from her when she would have held him there, eased the taut heat of his body lingeringly against hers, bringing his touch, his caress, his kiss, against her. Slowly.

The first time had been passion and anger.

This was to be passion and tenderness and caring.

And it was. He cherished her from her fingertips to her toes. He was in love with her feet, small and high-arched and beautiful. Her legs long and shapely and as smooth as silk. Her thighs, trembling to his touch. Hot velvet touches between them, and the erotic beauty of her response . . .

She whispered to him a dozen times, and a dozen times he told her no . . . and each plea was more fervent. Each touch of her fingers against him—down his chest, following the pattern of his hair, spanning his hips, cradling him intimately. Until the woman who had blushed at simple nudity was gone, and the true siren took her place, sensual, and so attuned to the pleasure to be shared that she was wanton, still innocently wanton . . .

Locked with him, above him, below him, sweet pulsing motion, fever and heat in the night. Beats throbbed throughout him, he'd held it so long . . . but then he felt the rocketing shudders of her body, the rush of warmth against him and he cast back his head, thrusting deep, shuddering violently.

He held her close, nuzzling against her hair. Tendrils of curls waved and tangled over his shoulders and chest and mesmerized him even as he cooled in aftermath.

"Come away with me," he whispered to her.

"Why do we need to go away?"

"Because I want you alone. Completely to myself. I want to watch you run naked on a beach. I want to—"

"Flynn!"

"Will you?"

And though she hesitated, this time she said "Yes."

The place they came to was a tiny island off the coast. There were only two houses there, one for the caretaker, and the other for them. Flynn told Brittany with a shrug that a number of people knew of its existence, then he laughed and told her which celebrities had rented the place and they speculated together whether the affairs that had taken place there had been legitimate or illicit.

"Can you cook?" Flynn asked her, showing her the small kitchen with its brick fireplace.

"Well, not gourmet."

"Edible?"

"I've survived this far."

"Thank God. We won't starve to death."

"I take it you don't cook?"

"Not for lack of effort. Maria says that I am capable of ruining boiling water."

"The luxuries of being rich!" Brittany teased him. "We peons must cook to eat. You should be grateful."

"Oh, I am grateful. And I really don't give a damn if you can cook or not . . ."

142

She found herself in his arms again, and a shiver touched her heart.

It was terrible to be this happy. Frightening.

He pulled away from her and caught her hand. "Come on, I'll show you the rest of our island."

It was beautiful. The sand was the whitest Brittany had ever seen. The inner island was covered with pines. Soft pines that offered shade, but though the sun was hot, there was always a breeze.

She never really needed to cook. The kitchen had come stocked with fruit and cheeses and breads and cold cuts and raw vegetables. The first hours they explored, but Brittany had come to know him, and she knew by the early afternoon that he was impatient and that they would see nothing else.

He'd meant what he said about the beach. It took some coaxing but he did convince her that there wasn't another living soul around so she shed her clothing along with him. They swam. They made love in the water, and then they made love out of the water and as the sun set, he quizzed her gently and she found herself telling him everything about her life.

"I don't suppose it's ever easy to lose one's parents. What haunted me the most was that my mother always hated those electric windows. Almost as if she knew . . ."

"Were they terribly young?"

Brittany, staring up at the magenta sky, shook her head against the sand. "My father was a scientist. A marine biologist. My mother was his assistant. She was almost forty when I was born. They loved their work, they loved one another."

"Then it was a good life. That's all that any of us can ask."

"I know."

"Why didn't you live with your aunt?"

Brittany turned in the sand, gazing at him with a curious smile. "How did you know that I didn't?"

"You lived with a family named Ericson."

"Mrs. Ericson was my mother's best friend. Mother had a will made, asking that I stay with them. Aunt Alice was already up in years, you know. She wanted me to come to London. But I was in high school, you know. I didn't think that I could bear to lose anything else at the time."

He came up on an elbow and touched her cheek.

"What else happened?"

"What do you mean?"

"Brittany, you're twenty-five, not eighteen, and—" He paused, grinning at her. "—ripe and luscious. What set of circumstances kept a young, independent American as pure as the driven snow all these years?"

She blushed uneasily and sat, wrapping her arms around her legs. "I was engaged to the Ericsons' son."

"And?"

She exhaled in a soft sigh.

"He died, too. In a boating accident."

"I'm sorry."

"So was I. I don't know if we were really right for one another or not. We were friends, though. Good friends."

"And you never—?"

" 'Mr.' Ericson was actually 'Reverend' Ericson. It was an old-fashioned household."

"When did your fiancé die?"

"Three years ago. After he died, I did go to stay with Alice for a while. She was such a wonderful woman, with such a marvelous outlook on life."

He sat too, slipping his arms over her shoulders, pulling her back against his chest. "Brittany, I promise you, we'll catch the man who caused her death. I promise."

She didn't reply. They sat there together until the breeze

144

suddenly shifted and Flynn warned her that it was going to rain and just then the drops began to fall.

They raced up to the house and Brittany proved that anyone could cook—she set out cold meats and cheese and grapes while Flynn started a fire.

Later that night they showered and lay before the dying embers in soft velvet robes, and while they sipped brandy, Brittany decided that it was her turn, she had a right to a few questions.

"What happened to your marriage?"

"It ended."

"Why?" Brittany persisted softly, and staring into the flames, Flynn shrugged.

"We were too young. I was twenty, Babs was nineteen. I was temperamental, she was a nag. She wanted to play the grand hostess, I wound up playing around. We were ill suited. She's a nice girl, and she likes me well enough now. When we chance to meet, we get along fine. We can laugh about the past."

"Could you always laugh?"

"No, I was quite bitter."

"Is that why you've avoided marriage all these years?"

"What kind of question is that?"

Brittany laughed and crawled up on his chest to stare down at him. "You forget, everything that I know about you has come from magazine stories. You avoid marriage, and you go through women like dish towels."

"I avoid dish towels."

"I'm sure you do. You haven't answered my question."

"I haven't avoided marriage. I asked you to marry me the other day, remember?"

"You didn't ask me. You said that you would do so with a horribly resigned air."

145

"Ah, but that's not fair. I wasn't playing with all the cards, my love." His eyes were silver—devil's eyes—wary and watchful and teasing all in one. "I thought that you were merely after my money. I didn't know that you would hurl my offer back as if I were indeed the Loch Ness Monster."

Brittany decided to wriggle away from him, but he caught her and dragged her back.

"Why is that?"

"Why is what?"

"Why is that you said you'd never marry me?"

"Because you weren't serious. You couldn't have been. I think you hated me."

He laughed, his eyes growing to dusky steel.

"I was dead serious. I told you, I'd crashed upon the rocks. If marriage was your price, I'd gladly have paid it."

"Price!" Brittany slammed a hand against his chest and he laughed again, seizing it.

"You were lying to me."

"Granted."

He shrugged. "So, have I gotten off cheaply? Or would you reconsider marriage?"

She hesitated, not knowing if he was teasing her or not.

"I don't think any sane woman would marry you, Flynn."

"Why?"

"Because it can't last."

"Why not?"

She lowered her lashes then raised them high again and faced him squarely.

"You want me now. You've apparently wanted any number of other women in your life." She paused. "And you've gotten them all."

"Brittany, I was bitter after I was divorced."

"How many women have you gone through, Flynn?" she

146

heard herself ask him a little bitterly. She couldn't help it. She felt the futility of it then. She felt as if she loved him desperately, and jealousy shot through her unbearably.

She couldn't help the feelings . . .

Flynn straightened up suddenly, dragging her onto his lap. He was tense and tight and his eyes flashed in the firelight.

"How many women? One a week following the divorce—is that what you want me to say? I don't know, Brittany. Your magazines were wrong, I never kept scorecards."

"What about Rosa?" she asked him softly.

A look of surprise and apology flashed quickly across his features.

"Yes, once. Long ago. It's been over for years. If you doubt that, ask Juan."

"Juan?"

"He intends to ask her to marry him soon, and I believe that she plans on saying yes. We're still good friends. Very good friends, but nothing more. Juan is my best friend, so I'll assume that you believe me."

"I—I believe you," she said.

"Are we done with twenty questions?"

"It wasn't anywhere near twenty questions!"

"Maybe not. Are we done?"

"Yes, damn you!"

"Good. Because your hair is pure copper in the firelight and I'm dying to see what it looks like against your naked flesh, and mine."

He kissed her slowly, leisurely. Her robe fell open and he slipped his hand inside, caressing her breast, flicking the nipple to a taut and aching peak.

He raised his head above hers intently for a moment.

"You forgot to ask one question, Brittany."

"I did?"

147

"I'll ask you. Do you love me?"

"I—"

"The truth."

"I—"

"Brittany?"

"Yes."

"I love you. And I haven't said that in over twelve years—no matter what you might have read in your magazines."

Her eyes widened. She didn't speak because he kissed her again and fire crackled and leapt in shadows across the wall and gave them soft warm light in which to make magical love.

CHAPTER EIGHT

The polo game was one of the most exciting events that Brittany had ever witnessed. Or maybe that was part of being in love, too. She didn't know who was more sleekly beautiful, Flynn, or the horse, Arabesque. She didn't understand a thing that was happening, though Elly Jones sat beside her and tried to explain. Polo was not a game to be understood from one watching. Ian received a penalty in the first chukker, which drew the time out to ten minutes and sent Elly into a righteous fit of anger. Ian was wonderful, Ian didn't deserve to be penalized—even if his Australian counterpart did have to go in for a new mount.

Juan, on Brittany's other side in the stands, cautioned Elly that rules were rules. Joshua Jones and his wife exchanged unhappy glances. Elly's crush on Ian was obvious and heart-wrenching to those older and wiser.

Is that how I appear? Brittany wondered. Had she entered into a fantasy world like Elly and refused to recognize how foolish she was being?

No, no, no, there was a massive difference. Flynn returned her feelings. She believed him. She believed in his promises.

"There'll be a break now," Juan told Brittany. "Shall I get you something? A glass of wine, a cold beer?"

The game was taking place in a covered stadium that was

filled with fans of numerous nationalities. The proceeds were to go to a children's foundation in Madrid, and Brittany was certain that they would be receiving a very large check—there were just so many wealthy people there.

There were men who walked along the stands with coolers, hawking their wares, like at a football game. There were no hot dogs and peanuts though; since the English were the host team, the food offerings were little pies and fried fish and fried potatoes offered with mayonnaise and vinegar. Brittany wasn't hungry in the least but she told Juan gratefully that she would love a glass of wine and when he left to find a vendor, she gazed at Elly.

"I'm going to be just like her!" Elly proclaimed suddenly, vehemently.

"Like who, Elly?"

"Rosa. Ian's going to teach me, and I'm going to play polo as well as she does. I'm more English than she is! When they need a third on an English team, it will be me—not her."

So Elly was jealous of Rosa, too, Brittany reflected. It was easy, the woman was beautiful, so full of life. Brittany hadn't been able to help herself from feeling rushes of envy since she knew that Rosa had once been with Flynn. But it was still hard to dislike Rosa, or let envy become bitter. She had congratulated Brittany so happily on the engagement, chided Flynn that there was no ring, and hugged them both. And of course, the way that Juan looked at her, the way that she returned that gaze . . .

You couldn't live in the past, Brittany told herself.

Nor could you let the future rule everything. Sometimes she shivered, wondering what she had done. Flynn kept insisting that he was working on her behalf, that he would corner the man she meant to catch. When she was with him, she believed in him. She believed that he loved her, she believed that things would work out in every direction. But the days were slipping by. Flynn left her now and then on business, but every time she was out he appeared. She tried to have lunch in town with the Joneses and he appeared there, ready to warn her when they left that she should take care. That he knew what he was doing, that she shouldn't be out with a suspect without him.

It was impossible to listen to him completely. This was her problem. And so she'd managed to take a casual ride over to Ian's for drinks and Flynn had appeared there again, and they'd had another row over it, but in the midst of the fight he'd suddenly stopped yelling and came to her, rimming her lips with a gentle touch of his thumb, reminding her that he loved her, and so she was still in love with him, still living with him, trusting him . . .

"But Flynn, nothing is happening!" she had told him once.

"My God, trust me, I'm doing everything in my power! You won't take me seriously until it's over and so believe me, I will find out who he is."

"Tell me what you're doing—"

"As soon as I can, I will."

At her side, Elly let out a sigh and leaned back in her seat, staring at the field. Brittany realized that Joshua and his wife had left the stands, and that Elly's sigh was of appreciation— her parents were gone.

"They are so horrid to me!" she wailed to Brittany.

"Elly, really, I'm sure they just want what's best."

"They think I'm too young for Ian."

You probably are, Brittany thought, but she didn't think that telling Elly that would be helpful in the least.

"Maybe they just feel that there are other men to meet, things to see, and a whole wonderful world open to a beautiful young eighteen-year-old," she told her instead.

Elly wrinkled her pretty features. "At least Father's going back to England on business. When he's out of the house, life is so much easier. Mother simply can't keep up with me. I get to breathe a bit. And things are always a bit better when he comes back. Financially, you know."

"Financially?"

"Surely. He trades, you know. He comes back with money!"

Brittany felt a little ill. If he came back with money, every time, he was doing something that was assured.

Something like stealing money from elderly investors . . .

"Father keeps whining that the business world is getting tougher and tougher and that things are moving in. Really, he's such a complainer. He hates to work, that's the true state of it. Oh! If I didn't have to wait three more years for that trust fund . . ."

Brittany smiled weakly at Elly. She thought that the young woman might profit very nicely herself from a brush with work. But she didn't say so. Not at that point.

"Tougher and tougher . . . moving in." Did Joshua Jones know that the police were closing in on him? Was he aware that the embezzler had been traced to the Costa del Sol? Did he know that he was not in the least safe anymore until he had touched down on Spanish soil?

She inhaled and exhaled, trembling slightly, anxious to talk with Flynn. She knew that he suspected Ian. He hadn't said so, she just knew it. But she believed that his suspicions had something to do with a rivalry that had been going on long before she had arrived upon the scene. She had suspected Ian herself. He was so smooth, so charming.

But now it seemed that it had to be Joshua. If one of them could just follow him. Or perhaps that wouldn't even be necessary. If she could find out when Joshua was leaving, where he would be staying, where he could be reached . . .

She could just call Brice and perhaps the police could close in on him when he was in the middle of another scam and then there would be proof and he could be prosecuted.

"Brittany?"

She turned. Juan had come back with her wine. She took it and thanked him and realized that he was watching her peculiarly.

"You're pale. Are you all right?"

"I'm fine, thank you." She smiled. She realized that the Joneses had taken their seats beside their daughter. She tried to stare at the field below. At the racing horses, at the excitement. At Flynn and Arabesque, graceful and fluid together.

She didn't see any of it. She knew only that the man who had killed her aunt was sitting three chairs away from her.

You have to be sure! she warned herself.

At last the game ended with the British group victorious. Brittany clapped along with the others, growing anxious as the crowd rose, as her view of Flynn was blocked. She had to reach him, she had to tell him what she knew about Joshua.

"Let's go down, shall we?" Juan said to her. And she nodded eagerly.

But when they reached the stables in the inner arena, only Rosa and Ian were there. Brittany congratulated Ian while Juan and Rosa met with a good-natured and dramatic kiss. Then Elly pushed by her to throw her arms around Ian, shrieking out how wonderful he was, how extraordinary, how handsome. Ian flushed, uneasily disentangling himself while watching Joshua Jones's eyes over his daughter's head.

"Rosa, where is Flynn?" Brittany was able to ask at last.

"Oh, Brittany. I'm sorry. He had to rush away. Business." She glanced at Juan, as if they shared some secret, making

153

Brittany very uneasy. "Juan must rush away too. I thought perhaps you would enjoy drinks and dinner with me. I know the loveliest sidewalk café. Will that be all right? I need only shower."

Brittany frowned. Flynn had disappeared quickly. Very quickly.

She bit her lip in frustration, then shrugged, moving slightly because Joshua Jones was very close behind her.

"I . . . suppose. But you needn't baby-sit me, Rosa. I can entertain myself, you know."

"Oh, no, no!" Rosa protested. "I would love dinner. Please, you must come with me. I'll shower now."

She kissed Juan quickly again, smiled, and disappeared. Brittany absently moved over to the stall where Arabesque stood and patted his smooth muzzle. She smiled slightly, for the animal's physical grace and beauty reminded her of its rider, and she was overwhelmed again with a cascade of emotions. It was terrible. Her feelings for him were so fierce, so desperate, and they could only lead to disaster.

It all had to come to an end—the quest for justice, the fevered affair. They were all tangled up together and the tension created made her feel that she was on a roller coaster and that if she was not careful, the car would slide from the tracks and she would hurl hopelessly into space and come crashing down . . .

"He's a beautiful animal, isn't he?"

She spun about. Joshua, smiling broadly, was standing next to her.

"Yes, he is."

Brittany tried very hard to speak lightly. She forced herself to smile. "He's actually Ian's horse, isn't he?"

"Yes. Flynn keeps trying to buy him. Ian hasn't given in yet, though."

154

"I hear you're going to London?"

"Yes." Joshua sighed. He shook his head. "I haven't a magical touch like Ian or Flynn." He gave off a broad, rocking laugh with bitter humor. "Or maybe they haven't a teen-aged daughter. I don't know."

He shook his head hopelessly. Brittany was almost drawn to sympathy. Was she wrong?

"I understand that you trade, Joshua. And deal in investments?"

"Deal in investments." He sniffed. Again he sounded bitter. "Well, yes, and my investments lately haven't been the best. That's my hope now, I've heard of a new company forming, with the stock going dirt cheap. Flynn is even up on this one. He says it can't fail."

"Flynn?"

Icy little rivulets scampered down her spine. Flynn? In it with Joshua. No. She couldn't believe it. She had to be wrong, wrong from the start. Joshua was innocent, and so was Flynn . . .

Things were going to get better, Elly had told her. They always did when her father went to London.

She couldn't see suddenly. She couldn't see clearly. She felt that she had to get away. That she had to reason things out.

"Excuse me, Joshua, will you?"

She pushed past him blindly. She didn't want to be with Rosa, she didn't want to be with anyone. She wanted to rush out and find a cab and have him take her away from all these people, away to some private place where she could think it all out . . .

She crashed into Ian and paled, not wanting to be delayed from leaving.

"Brittany!" He caught her shoulders. "I'm so sorry. It's just that I'm in such a rush . . ."

155

"I'm sorry; I crashed into you."

"No, no. I've just got to hurry . . ."

He stepped past her. No delay there. She saw that Rosa had reappeared in a charming white dress that enhanced all her dark beauty.

Brittany stepped behind a boisterous group of Spaniards. Then she turned and ran for the entrance to the arena, rushing outside as fast as she could.

There were taxis everywhere, but there were people too. She kept dodging around them, running farther and farther along the street. The farther away from the entrance that she came, the more likely she might find a free cab.

She found one. The driver was a young man with a beautiful white-toothed grin—who didn't understand a word of English. Brittany thought for a moment and gave him Flynn's name and the word *casa*, and that he did seem to understand.

The water was what she needed, she had decided. She could take one of the small craft out and be totally alone at sea and there she could desperately try to unravel everything that she knew.

The cab driver let her off in front of the house. Brittany didn't go in. She walked around the great *casa* to the dock in the back.

She felt stiff, awkward, disjointed—as if even walking were an alien chore. Something burned inside of her, something aching and horrible that brought crimson humiliation and fury to seethe inside her.

She had fallen in love with him. Easily. For everything that she had known and read, she had been with him barely a week before the desire had killed all sense and logic. Like a totally naïve fool she had fallen in love with him and given him everything. And it seemed now that he was in on it. She had known that it had to have been one of three people, but

156

she had fallen in love with him anyway, with his husky voice, his sleek broad shoulders, his smooth and practiced seduction that had taken her . . .

No! she cried out to herself. She didn't really know anything. She knew that Joshua was going to London. That things always got better when he went to London. That Flynn was in on this one with him. No, she couldn't be wrong. She had poured out her heart to him. She had given him all the details of her lost and barren little life and she had been as pathetic as putty in his hands.

He could be laughing at her. Laughing at her so hard. Listening to her story and pretending and enjoying the whole thing because even if she did know the truth, there wouldn't be a thing that she could do, not unless she could get him back onto English soil and not even then could she do anything unless she had proof . . .

It wasn't Flynn. Her heart cried out that it wasn't Flynn. And then the most logical sense of it all came to her. No, it wasn't Flynn. He had been going in league with Joshua just now in order to trap him—in order to get him to England so that he could be arrested!

Brittany stopped short on the dock before approaching the little fleet that included the yacht and the catamarans and . . .

A boat she had never seen before.

It was painted indigo. In the coming darkness, it almost blended in entirely with the water. There was no name upon it; it was almost like a ghost ship. It was a power boat, about forty-five feet long, with a set of ropes and grappling hooks set along the side.

She was too stunned at first to even begin to imagine what the boat was doing there. Numbed, she approached it. Still not

157

thinking, she doffed her heels and hopped aboard in her stocking feet.

She looked at all the ropes and the grappling hooks and admitted in her mind long before she could do so in her heart that the appearance of the nameless craft could only mean one thing.

It had to be a pirate ship. *The* pirate ship playing havoc on the coast. Indigo like the water, like the horizon. A ship that could sneak upon other ships and prey upon them. It was the right size; it would have the speed. It was laden with all the equipment needed to hold fast to another vessel while that victim boat was ravaged and stripped.

"Oh, God," Brittany breathed aloud.

And she looked around herself quickly, very quickly. There was no one about the dock. Tears stung her eyes with the deep horror of being able to find no denial.

It was here! Berthed at Flynn's docks, among his ships. There was no way that he couldn't know it was here. Of course he knew; he used it; it was his indigo privateer.

Flynn was an embezzler, a crook—and a pirate. He had known who she was from the very beginning because he had known damned well that El Drago hadn't attacked her—because he was El Drago himself. She had slept with the man who was responsible for her aunt's death. The man who was ravaging the seas.

She pressed her hands against her cheeks and remembered with horror all the intimacies that they had shared. How she had blushed but then laughed and learned and come to him with whispers and cries on her lips, abandoning all dignity.

She drew her hands away and swallowed tensely, then reminded herself coldly that she was on El Drago's ship and that there might well be some proof against him on it. The British government might be very interested in discovering

158

proof against the pirate ravaging the property of Britons. If she could continue to play the innocent, she could lure him back to England. If the Spanish police might be interested in doing something; El Drago was a Spanish menace.

Brittany hurried to the short flight of steps that led to the cabin below. The wheel of the motor craft was forward; the hatch and steps were just before it. She noted uneasily that the sky was very dark. She hurried below deck anyway.

The galley was first, a small area with little attention given to the needs of cooking. There was a counter, a small stove top and a small refrigerator. Right behind it was a chart desk and it was there that Brittany hurried. But though she rummaged through the drawers, there was nothing there. Nothing but charts that warned of the islands and shoals and currents that surrounded the coast.

Islands . . .

Like the little island where he had taken her. Where they had run naked on the beach. Made love on the sand. Where she had given him the wasteland of her past, and believed him when he had told her that he loved her . . .

Nothing.

She sat down at the table and looked down the hallway and realized that there were cabins beyond. She rushed down the hallway and found that the first wooden door led to a little cabin. Very small in size, but still that of the captain, she was certain. It housed a bunk and another desk.

She started quickly through the desk and found paper that contained dates . . . and lists. She read it over and over— and found with increasing horror the exact date that her aunt had died. With a cross reference to the exact amount of money embezzled from her.

Brittany let the paper fall to the floor, and stared after it. She fell back on the bunk and knew that the other dates

159

and amounts must relate to the other elderly people who had been swindled.

Someone had been taken just two days ago.

Two days ago, when Flynn had been out all day, well into the night, on business.

She inhaled and it was a sob and she slipped her arms around her knees and rocked back and forth. And then suddenly, she realized that the night had come alive with sound.

The motor was running.

Like lightning she came to her feet and rushed to the door. She came silently down the hallway and stood in the galley, staring silently up the stairs.

At the helm were two men and a woman. The woman, Brittany quickly realized, was Rosa.

"I'm sorry! I don't know what happened! She was very agreeable—but then she was gone! Perhaps she is up at the house. Perhaps—"

"Rosa! I searched the house!"

It was Flynn. Brittany squinted against the darkness that was only alleviated by dimmed cruising lights.

The other man was at the wheel; Flynn was facing Rosa. He was dressed entirely in black. Black jeans, black turtleneck, black scarf around his throat. He looked like a lethal panther, muscled and dark. One with the night. Ready to strike. A pirate . . .

He turned suddenly, saying something to Rosa about checking below. Rosa said she would go back to the house and wait for Brittany.

They were all in on it. Oh, God! All of them. Flynn and Rosa and Juan and Joshua. Ian was quite probably the only innocent man of her acquaintance.

Flynn started toward the steps.

Brittany panicked. He wasn't expecting her—not here. If she could only find something . . .

There was a frying pan hung on a hook behind the stove top. She raced silently for it, grappled with the hook, and grabbed it, her heart racing like thunder. She freed it from the hook and retreated down the hall, shaking. Her only chance against him was the element of surprise.

Or should she hide? Simply hide and ride it out and try to get the slip that proved that he had been involved with every date and time.

He was on the last step when she slipped back into the cabin, quietly closing the door behind her. The paper was on the floor where it had fallen. Brittany grasped it and slipped it into the pocket of her denim skirt and then held still, listening, the frying pan gripped so tightly in her fingers that they ached with the pressure.

She gasped softly because she realized that he was coming down the hallway. The cabin was so small . . .

She opened the wardrobe and realized that she would never fit within it. There was a door at the rear of the cabin, she dashed for it and discovered that it was the head. Small—but large enough to shelter her.

She closed that door just as she heard the outer one opening.

Her breathing seemed ridiculously harsh and loud; she could have even sworn that her heartbeat was thunder, that it could be heard above the hum of the motor.

She waited, waited and waited, so tense.

And then finally, she heard the outer door open and close. She leaned against the head door, feeling ill, wondering desperately just what she should do. If she attempted to stop him, she would probably fail. She would find herself in danger—

and what proof she had against him would be wrested from her.

But could she do nothing? Could she let him take to the seas and ravage some innocent ship?

El Drago didn't hurt people; he didn't kill them. He only stole from them. Rosa had even said that he was a gentleman. But of course, Rosa was in on it with him. She had helped El Drago clean out Ian's boat.

The head was stifling. So hot and close that she couldn't breathe. She had to come out. Perhaps she could reason more easily with more air.

Brittany twisted the knob as silently as she could and started out, then froze.

He was waiting for her. Casually leaned against the desk, arms crossed. Eyes shimmering a cool silver and cutting into her.

Instinct and blind panic prevailed. He started toward her and she swung out with her frying pan.

He was too quick; he caught her wrist and though she struggled, his grip upon her wrist was so tight that she cried out at last, releasing her weapon.

"Brittany—"

"Get your hands off me!" she shrieked. "Let me go. Oh, my God, I hate you, I can't believe—"

"Brittany! It isn't what you think!"

She could feel him. Feel him hot and towering over her. The muscles in his chest, in his arms, hard and steeled and powerful against her. She felt his subtle scent surround and invade her and she feared that she would pass out.

She had loved him—loved him desperately. Touched him and explored and learned by her hands. She knew the physique that held her prisoner now so achingly well . . .

"Oh, God!"

She struggled in panic and fury against him and he grimly tried to subdue her and talk at the same time.

"Brittany, I'm telling you that you don't—"

"You're El Drago! Don't deny it!"

"Yes, I am, but—"

"You bastard! All this time! You were going to help me! I had to watch out for Ian, I had to watch out for Joshua, I was supposed to trust you, I was—oh, God!"

"Brittany, I didn't—"

"You're El Drago, and you're an embezzler—and a murderer!"

"Damn it—"

"I have the proof!"

She wrenched against him with such a great fury that she took him by surprise and freed herself, then wished fervently that she hadn't spoken. She had never seen him look more grim, more hostile.

More cold or ruthless.

He backed away from her slightly. She thought of bolting for the door, but knew that he would stop her. And if he didn't, his accomplice would be above on deck . . .

They couldn't be that far from shore yet. If she could escape, she could swim to freedom.

"Where's the proof?" he asked her softly.

She shook her head.

He smiled, but she didn't like the cast of that smile. It was bitter and mocking. He didn't come toward her. He just stared at her. "You told me that you loved me."

"I was a fool, wasn't I? I played into your hands so easily!"

"Love means trust, Brittany."

She started to laugh. "You are El Drago! You just told me so!"

163

"It isn't what it seems. Now, what proof are you talking about?"

It was now or never. She bolted for the door and threw it open and raced down the hallway. He followed, right on her heels. She made it up the steps just ahead of him.

The man turned from the wheel. It was Juan. Brittany stared at him; he stared at her with stunned surprise.

Thankfully, he was so surprised that she was able to race past him to the starboard rail, leap upon it, pose—and dive.

The sea was dark; pitch dark. As black as ink as she submerged deep, stroked desperately, and swam as far as her lungs would carry her, beneath the surface.

Her skirt was dragging her down. The weight of the denim was too much for a midnight swim. Brittany reached into the pocket for the all-important paper and prayed that it would survive the water. She slipped it beneath her bra strap and kicked away the denim.

And even then, she felt his arms. He'd found her.

It was a deadly game, a game they'd played once before. She could escape him. She could escape almost any hold in the water. But he could catch her. Again and again. Every time.

His grip came around her; she jackknifed downward and eluded him. But when she surfaced, gasping for air, he was there, just feet from her, treading water.

"Brittany! I did not swindle your aunt! I am El Drago, but you don't understand. I'm not really a pirate—"

"Oh, no. That's right. You're Robin Hood. You really work for the Spanish police, right? Or is it the British?"

Sarcasm laced her voice and she wondered if she wasn't crazy. If he did catch her now . . .

He was curiously silent, watching her. She pitched herself downward again, deep, and began to swim, desperate.

164

And then he caught her in a hold that she could not escape. His fingers wound tight into her hair. So tight that she tried to scream and gulped in water instead. He brought her to the surface. He used his hold upon her hair to drag her back to the ship. She was still coughing and panting and exhausted when Juan reached overboard, dragging her up while Flynn caught hold and crawled over the rail.

Juan didn't pay the least bit of attention to her, except to cast her a sorry gaze. His anxious attention was entirely for Flynn.

"She's right off the starboard bow. We've got to cut the lights."

Flynn nodded, running his fingers quickly through his soaked hair, then reaching for the deck to grab Brittany's hand.

"I'll just see to our guest," he said dryly.

He tried to pull her to her feet; when she kicked and flailed and clawed at him and with an oath of vast impatience, he simply reached down for her and threw her over his shoulder, balancing easily, even with her protesting weight, as he moved down the stairs.

He pushed her into the cabin. She backed away, aware that she was drenched and ill clad in her shirt and stockings and panties. He arched a brow while he cast his eyes over her with some amusement and then she screamed as he unbuckled his belt and whipped it away from his waistline.

Her scream didn't divert him in the least. He stepped toward her and she put up a hand to ward him off, he caught it and slipped the belt around it, securing her other hand to tie with the first, and then looped the end around the post to the bunk. Shivering, miserable, Brittany tried hard to stare at him with dignity and loathing. He wouldn't really hurt her. He wouldn't hurt her, but she was afraid . . .

"You bastard. Rat bastard," she spat out at him.

"I'm sorry that you see it that way," he said softly. He touched her cheek and she tried to wrench away from him.

"Brittany," he murmured softly. "I just don't have time now. But I will take that proof."

A little gasp escaped her. He reached into her bra and fumbled for the paper. Her flesh burned as she felt his touch. A touch that despite everything had become so a part of her that she shivered, hated herself, shivered again . . .

He smiled and saluted her.

"I'll be back, Brittany," he promised. "I really am sorry for the inconvenience, but you don't want to listen, you don't want to believe me."

"Go to the devil, El Drago," she snapped.

He watched her for a moment. She didn't know what was in his eyes. Pain, disappointment? Something wistful, even . . .

But then he laughed at the horror in her expression and the sound was harsh.

"I will be back," he promised her.

After tying a handkerchief over her mouth, he turned silently. And left her.

CHAPTER NINE

It was impossible for anyone to create such a binding knot with a leather belt; the more Brittany worked at it, the more she struggled, the more tightly she found herself held.

She worked feverishly, twisting her wrists, utilizing her teeth, and all to no avail. She thought she finally had a good bite upon a piece that would give when she was suddenly jolted hard against the bunk.

She paused, aware of a harsh, grinding sound. She realized that they had come alongside another boat.

At first she heard nothing. Then she heard shouts, an argument—and a woman's tears.

El Drago had struck again, Brittany thought bitterly.

But the boat was still. She got a good hold upon the belt again with her eyeteeth. Tears came to her eyes and the leather threatened to gag her but she kept at it anyway. It seemed to be slipping at last. If she could wedge the loop free . . .

She halted, frozen, the loop in her mouth. Someone was coming to the powerboat. She heard first a heavy thud of footsteps, then she heard a woman's shrill voice.

"I'll never forgive you, Flynn. Never! As long as I live. I'll find you. I'll—"

"Stop it, Elly. Just stop it."

It was Flynn's voice that time. Tired, resigned. Elly burst into tears. Brittany groaned as a swift knifing of agony seemed to shear through her. Flynn was comforting Elly, pulling her to his chest to muffle her sobs, probably smoothing back her soft blond hair . . .

Elly, Elly! she thought. In love with Ian who would never really love her in return, so accustomed to Flynn's autocracy that when she recognizes him for the pirate that he is, he can still soothe and subdue her . . .

"Come on," Flynn said softly.

Brittany heard their footsteps again. Flynn walked her by the door to the first cabin.

She heard a second door shut, then more footsteps. Footsteps that paused at her door, then moved on toward the ladder again.

Brittany closed her eyes and swallowed. He was holding Elly prisoner, too. If she could just slip the knot, she could free them both . . .

She started at it again with the determination of a beaver. Time seemed to tick away relentlessly, but she had heard nothing more than a continuation of Elly's soft sobbing when she finally slipped the loop, wrenched and wriggled, and freed her hands. Then she undid the handkerchief about her mouth.

She gasped with relief and rubbed her wrists quickly, then hurried to the door. She opened it, and looked carefully in both directions, then hurried down the hall. The sobbing was coming from the second door. Brittany expected to find it locked; it was not. Poor Elly . . . Flynn didn't even think of her as a danger. Just shut her up and get her out of the way.

"Elly!"

Brittany threw open the door. Elly was just sitting on the bunk. Her eyes were swollen and red-rimmed but she gulped and stopped crying and stared at Brittany wide-eyed when she heard her name called.

"Brittany!"

"Shh, Elly! He'll know that I'm loose."

Elly kept staring, then she started laughing a little ridiculously.

"You look like a wet burlesque dancer," Elly told her.

"What difference does it make what I look like?" Brittany demanded impatiently. "We've got to stop him!"

"Wh-at?" Elly said, slowly, carefully.

"Who were you with? Ian?"

With a little jerk, Elly nodded.

"Flynn is still on the boat with him?"

Again, Elly nodded. Brittany bit uncertainly into her lower lip. "We've got to stop him."

Elly suddenly flew to her feet, her eyes bright with elation. She threw her arms around Brittany. "Oh, yes! Come on, I know exactly what to do!"

"Wait, Elly, wait! He could be dangerous. I don't know if he's armed or not, he must have something to be able to get away with this all the time. We have to—"

"He's got Ian handcuffed," Elly said with a sniff. "He's just going through the boat now. He won't expect us, and I know where Ian's gun is!"

Elly started out but Brittany grabbed her arm. "Elly, wait. What about Juan?"

"He's tearing apart all of Ian's crates, too. Come on, Brittany! We'll stop him!"

Elly hurried down the hallway and Brittany followed her, still shushing her and warning her to be cautious. But Elly was right; there was no one topside on Flynn's indigo pirate ship, nor was anyone above the deck on Ian's sailing yacht beside it. The grappling hooks were all in place and they were easily able to hop from deck to deck. Elly was dressed for it in Topsiders and jeans. Brittany's stockinged feet were less appropriate and Elly paused again to giggle at how ridiculous she looked which irritated Brittany no end. Was Elly too immature to realize the precariousness of their positions? Or even what all this meant? All she seemed to know was that Flynn was abusing her beloved Ian.

"This way!" Elly told Brittany—and this time she was the one to draw a finger to her lips for silence.

It was a dark night. Not even the stars were out. But the lights inside the yacht were ablaze when Elly led Brittany down a short flight of elegantly carpeted steps to the below deck. Here they didn't enter a half-stocked galley, but an elegant salon with a warm wood card table and luxurious settees soldered hard to the teak paneling.

Elly tiptoed to the card table and pulled out one of the side drawers that should have contained poker chips. It held a small silver pistol instead.

"Is it loaded?" Brittany asked her nervously.

"Of course," Elly said grimly.

"Maybe I should take it," Brittany said nervously. She didn't want Elly shooting Flynn in cold blood. She wanted Flynn to go back to England. She wanted him to stand trial. She wanted them to lock him away for years and years, until he was so old that he could never seduce a little old lady out of her money again, or a foolish young one into loving him . . .

"I'll keep it," Elly insisted. "Shh!"

Brittany became aware of voices then. Juan's voice, first, she thought. And he was speaking in rapid Spanish. To Flynn she was certain. She heard bitter laughter—Ian's, probably. He told Flynn that he could go to hell, adding, "I should have known. I should have known that you were the ever-illustrious El Drago."

170

Elly gripped Brittany's arm fiercely. She swallowed nervously. "They're right through that door. In the captain's cabin. You throw it open; I'll hold the gun on them."

Brittany still wasn't sure that she liked Elly having the gun, but there really wasn't any time to waste. Even having the gun, she wouldn't feel safe against Flynn once he was forewarned of their presence.

She nodded and together the girls edged toward the door. They both swallowed. Elly looked at her with wide, pleading eyes.

Brittany nodded again. Elly stepped back and she threw the door open.

"Freeze right where you are, Flynn Colby! You, too, Juan. I swear, I'll shoot you if I have to!" Elly swore.

Three pair of incredulous eyes trained on the two of them. Ian was sitting on the large masted bed that occupied a large portion of the cabin—and he was handcuffed, as Elly had said. He also had a bruise about his eye which promised to be a shiner by morning. He looked sullen and irritable. Brittany noticed that the sheets were mussed and that Ian was minus his shirt and she presumed that Flynn's piracy had interrupted his and Elly's lovemaking.

Juan and Flynn were in the corner of the cabin, opening a set of packing boxes. Hunched down on the balls of their feet, they stared as blankly as Ian did.

Ian looked from Brittany with surprise and a smile to Elly. "Well bless your hearts, luvs," he murmured. "Hold that gun steady, Elly. Tell Flynn to get these things off me. Tell him you'll shoot him in the kneecaps if he doesn't. I should have the gun, Elly."

Elly looked nervously from Ian to Flynn. Juan didn't move. He kept staring at Elly. Flynn cast Brittany one scathing glance, then stood, locking his eyes with Elly's.

"Flynn! You heard him!" Elly's voice rose high and shrill. "Take the cuffs off him!"

Flynn didn't move. He set his hands on his hips and stared at Elly.

"You don't want me to do that," he told her softly.

"Yes, she does!" Brittany suddenly screeched. What was he, an idiot? Oh, God, she wanted him locked away. She didn't want to see him standing there, staring Elly down when Elly was holding the gun with trembling fingers.

After all this . . .

Oh, what a fool she was, because she knew that she wouldn't be able to bear it if Elly did pull the trigger, if she put a bullet hole in Flynn's broad chest, if he fell to the floor in a pool of blood . . .

And the stupid, stupid man! He was standing there, calm, deadly calm, watching Elly. Glancing quickly at Brittany with eyes that sizzled out a hard silver warning, as if he were still the one in charge, as if El Drago could defy bullets.

"Flynn . . ." Elly said. Her voice was growing weaker.

He took a step toward her, slowly, reaching out a hand.

"Elly, dammit, shoot him!" Ian shouted.

Brittany inhaled, trembling miserably. Flynn took another step toward Elly. Elly told him to stop. The gun shook in her outstretched hands.

Brittany was terrified that Elly would pull the trigger.

She was equally afraid that she would not; that Flynn would never be afraid of her, that what they had done would only make things worse. They all knew who Flynn was, and that Juan was a conspirator. Could Flynn afford to let them live?

"Elly, Elly!"

She cried out the words herself and made a sudden swoop toward the girl, wrenching the gun from the shaking fingers, holding it herself on Flynn and backing away from him. Elly

172

cried out in a little sob and sank down to the carpeting, crying softly. Ian started to say something to her; Brittany didn't hear it. She couldn't even see the others. All she saw was Flynn. He stared at her now. And he didn't pause. He kept coming toward her, too, reaching for the gun.

"Brittany, give it to me. You don't know what you're doing."

"Flynn, get back. I'm not eighteen and I swear I don't want to hurt you, but Ian is right, if I shoot your kneecap, you'll survive, but you'll do so in a great deal of pain."

He did pause then. He stared at her. Then he spun around, staring toward the bed, shouting, "What was that?"

Surely, surely, it was the oldest trick in the book.

And Brittany fell for it. Her eyes followed his warning, and in those split seconds, he made a dive for her. She was suddenly flat on the floor with his weight over her, his face grim, his mouth a line as he shook her wrist, tensing his hold, until she dropped the pistol.

Then he smiled icily. "Thank you."

He stood up, dragging her along with him, keeping a twist lock on her arm so that she couldn't begin to escape him. "Juan," he murmured, sounding weary, "Juan, *amigo*, can you handle things this side until the troops arrive?"

Juan gazed down at Elly, who was still crying softly on the floor. He gazed toward Ian—silent and hostile. He shrugged and grinned at Flynn.

"*Sí.*"

Then he gazed at Brittany and smiled broadly. "*Sí,*" he repeated.

Brittany winced as Flynn forced her to turn about and prodded her back through the salon, and up the steps.

"Where are we going now?" she demanded harshly.

173

"Should I make you walk the plank?" he queried at her earlobe.

"I really don't see one," she replied coolly. It couldn't be happening. Why did her heart still pound? How could she still think that the subtle scent he carried was pleasant and alluring and sexual . . .

He was probably going to kill her. He would be charming until the very end. She would be torn like this until she drew her last breath . . .

No. She stiffened. He wasn't a cold-blooded murderer. He would probably set them adrift and disappear. Somewhere else. Down to Africa, perhaps.

"Let's go, my little mermaid. Back to my—uh—pirate ship."

She really didn't have any choice. When she balked, he picked her up bodily and scissored his legs from deck to deck with her in his arms.

Fear enveloped her when he headed straight down the steps and back to the cabin where she had been his prisoner. She stiffened, and when he kicked the door open, she panicked. She tried to twist and flail against him but he laughed and cast her down to the bunk and then fell upon her, his weight trapping her, his wet clothing soaking through the sheer damp fabric she had left to clothe her. She stared at him, frightened, hating him . . .

Still in disbelief. He was so arresting. Dark and dangerously handsome and alluring and she had fallen in love with a thief . . .

"Why didn't you shoot?"

"What?"

"Why didn't you shoot? You had the chance."

She squirmed beneath his weight. She would never shift

174

him, and she knew it. She only succeeded in bringing them closer and closer.

She lifted her chin.

"I didn't wish to kill you in cold blood."

"That was noble of you."

"I would now," she promised.

He smiled, lowered his lashes, and brought his hand to her cheek. "Would you really?"

"I would! And stop that!"

"Why?"

"I despise you! You killed my aunt! You've robbed time and time again and—"

"You don't despise me. You would have shot me," he whispered softly.

"I do despise you," she swore, and then she went hastily silent because a sob threatened in her voice and at this late date, she swore she wasn't going to be a coward where he was concerned.

"You still don't see . . ." he whispered. "Oh well."

He sat up suddenly, pulling his damp black shirt over his shoulders and casting it aside. Brittany looked at him in horror.

"What are you doing?" she rasped out.

He stared at her, smiling broadly. For all the world like a true pirate, victorious after hauling a great booty.

But then he was victorious, wasn't he?

"Well, I'm a pirate, aren't I?" he asked her, quite naturally. He stood, and in utter amazement, she stared at him. His shoulders were damp and glowing in that sleekness. All the sinews and muscles of his shoulders and chest were sharply delineated and all his power seemed evident.

And all she could do was stare . . .

He smiled again, sat at the edge of the bed even as she

crept as high and tight as she could against the headboard. He cast off his squeaking sneakers and socks and then stood, and even as she gasped, he grimaced, and struggled out of his wet black jeans.

He leaned over her and smiled again.

"Pirates ravish people, you know," he told her lightly.

"I'll scream!" she promised him stupidly.

He shrugged. What the hell difference did it make?

But he didn't touch her. He walked, easy and comfortable in his nudity—and why not? They had been together easy and comfortable that way dozens of times—and went over to the wardrobe.

He drew out a new pair of worn jeans and slid into them, his back to her. He found a yellow knit shirt and slipped that over his head and then returned to the wardrobe, producing a terry robe which he tossed to her.

"Put that on." He grinned. "That's the most outlandish outfit I've ever seen. I might rather like it myself. I've always been fond of garters. But you look like a stripper out of some little joint on 42nd Street in the Big Apple."

The robe landed on her lap. Brittany looked from the robe to Flynn in astonishment.

"I'm sorry—did I disappoint you? If I'm supposed to ravish you, I'll gladly oblige. Really I—"

He paused suddenly, listening. Then he snapped his fingers.

"Sorry, Ms. Martin. Your ravishment will have to wait."

Ignoring her, he turned around and left her in the cabin. Free. And the door was open.

Hopelessly confused and aching, Brittany bounded from the bunk and followed him. He was up on deck—and a third vessel was coming alongside them. A man in white was waving to Flynn.

"Everything all right?"

"Fine," Flynn shouted back. He noticed that Brittany was behind him. "Want to cast over a line, there, Brit?"

"What?"

Juan made an appearance on the deck of Ian's yacht. "Eh, *amigo!* How's it going?"

"Great—we've got the big fish!"

Brittany found that her knees didn't hold her anymore. They buckled, and she found herself sitting on the deck, staring as the boats came together, as the lines were thrown and drawn, as the gray-haired man with the very proper British accent came hopping from deck to deck.

He glanced at her curiously, smiled, but offered his hand quickly to Flynn. Juan hopped from boat to boat, and shook hands with the gray-haired man, too.

"We've got everything?" he asked then, a little anxiously.

Flynn nodded. "The jewelry is all in the crate in Drury's cabin. It's what we've been waiting for. A definite connection."

The gray-haired man nodded, made a motion toward his own ship, and was joined by two other men who nodded at Flynn and Juan but did not stop to chat—they proceeded on to Ian's yacht and disappeared below.

"Well, that's it, then. We can't tarry long," the gray-haired man said, "we're not really in international waters. We've got to move out. I promise drinks and dinner as soon as you're back in London, though. Juan, *amigo*, you must take a vacation, too."

"*Sí*, I think that I will," Juan said. He looked at Brittany, grinning. "*Sí*, I think that I will make it to London for the wedding."

"Wedding?"

The gray-haired man turned back to Brittany with surprise,

then he stared at Flynn with astonishment and came over to Brittany, helping her back up to her feet.

"Chief Ellsworth Harrington, Brittany Martin—my fiancée," Flynn explained. "Oh—and if you need help at the trial . . . well, you know. I told you about her aunt. Alice Whalen."

"Oh, yes," Ellsworth Harrington said. He patted Brittany's hand. "I'm sorry, lass, truly sorry. If we should need your help—?"

She couldn't speak. She was still too confused to speak. She nodded.

"London then!" Harrington said. He squeezed Brittany's hand again, then dropped it easily. He saluted Flynn and started back for his own craft. One of the other men appeared topside of Ian's yacht with Elly Jones in tow.

"Colby!" he called out to Flynn. "Am I supposed to take this one too?"

"No, she's not guilty of anything but lovesickness," Flynn called back. Juan moved to help Elly from Ian's yacht to Flynn's little powerboat. Flynn gazed over at Brittany, his eyes shimmering now with humor.

"It's a rather hopeless disease," he said softly, for her ears only, "with definitely dangerous potential."

Ellsworth Harrington shouted to his men to cast off. Flynn stopped gazing at Brittany to free Ian's yacht and Harrington's craft from his own. Juan held Elly; the four of them silent while the other ships moved until they blended in with the velvet-and-ink darkness of the night.

Elly was still crying. Flynn turned to her, gently.

"Elly, you have to understand," he told her with quiet patience. "He was hurting people. Really hurting them—"

Elly didn't let him finish. She tore from Juan and threw herself against Flynn's chest.

"I'm sorry, Flynn. I'm sorry, I didn't want to believe you, I didn't—Flynn, I could have shot you. Flynn . . . ?"

"Elly," he said. "You didn't shoot me. That's what is important." He smoothed blond hair from her forehead and smiled. "We won't tell your dad a thing, huh? Why don't you go down to the galley and get yourself a glass of wine and maybe take a little nap while we head back in, huh?"

Elly nodded. Tears were welling in her eyes again. When she turned around and had to face Brittany, she started crying all over again.

"I'm—I'm sorry, Brittany. I—uh—I knew then, but when I saw you, I thought that I could save Ian."

"It's all right, Elly."

Elly went on down the stairs. Juan murmured that he would get her something to drink, and followed her.

The indigo boat sat silently on the dark sea and night swept around them. Brittany felt the salt air on her cheeks, cool and caressing. Cool when she felt so very hot. He was staring at her with a mixture of tenderness and amusement. Staring at her with a query in his high-arched brow.

"What—what just happened?" she asked softly at last.

"Well, I was a pirate. Sort of," Flynn said, taking a step toward her. "But Ian was the man that you wanted. They've been watching his coming and goings from the home office for a long time now."

"You're a—policeman?"

"No. Not exactly."

"You're with the CIA?"

Flynn chuckled softly, taking another step toward her.

"No. That's an American agency. I work for the British government, but if you had called your friend Brice, you wouldn't have been able to clarify anything. They would have had to deny me. It's a sticky situation, you see. Spanish officials don't necessarily want to shield British criminals. Their hands are often tied. But neither could they really condone a pirate off the coast and the only way we could ever really haul Ian into court was to have some tangible proof against him so I had to rifle a few of his boats. The rest of the legend . . ." He shrugged, grinning, and took his last step toward her, setting his hands upon her shoulders.

"There really wasn't such a thing as the El Drago you claimed to have attacked you at sea. We all created the legend. There were a couple of other instances when the pirate did go to sea. We had a bank clerk down here who had embezzled a couple of million pounds and Juan and I came aboard to find those pounds and transfer them back. Other than that . . ."

"Rosa knew," Brittany said. "Rosa knew all along."

"Well, yes. She's the one who managed to create the legend for the newspapers."

Brittany shook her head. "You knew! You knew from the moment that I opened my mouth that I hadn't been attacked by El Drago because you were El Drago!"

"Well, yes."

Brittany lowered her head.

"Tonight—" she whispered.

"You're a real little horror, you know that, my love? I asked you to trust me—"

"You scared me half to death in there!"

"Only because you chose not to trust me!"

"Oh, my God," Brittany murmured, gripping his arms because her knees were trembling again. "Flynn, I held a gun on you. I could have shot you. I brought Elly out to get that gun. Elly could have shot you—and you, you stupid idiot! You just stood there and you could have been—"

He laughed softly. It seemed to be part of the velvet of the night, and she couldn't believe that the night could have come out this way, beautiful, the two of them here, together, alive and well, and—innocent.

"Brittany, I've known Elly a long time. I knew that she was never going to pull that trigger."

"She might have panicked."

"Sometimes you have to gamble. I thought that it was a safe bet. But, now, as to you—"

"How did you know that I wouldn't pull the trigger?"

"Because I knew that you still loved me, even if you were doing a fabulous job at denial."

"You knew that I loved you—still?"

"Mm-hmm." He moved even closer. Brittany felt his body hard and flush against hers, warm and stirring and wonderful.

"How?"

"Your eyes."

"Oh, really?"

"Mm-hmm."

"You faltered—because you loved me."

"No—I didn't falter. You disarmed me."

"I faltered."

"You did?"

"Hmm. I almost lost everything because I loved you. I couldn't tell you the whole truth because there were others involved and because the home office doesn't trust anyone. But then suddenly there you were in the thick of things and I was trying so desperately to explain when I should have been paying more attention to what El Drago was up to. And then, of course, I underestimated you. I was so anxious to have it all over with and try again to explain, that I wasn't in the least prepared for you and Elly to arrive in Ian's cabin. I couldn't think . . ."

He kissed her forehead, the tip of her nose, and then her lips, softly.

"El Drago is gone for good, you know. He never really was such a bad guy. So—are you going to marry me?"

Brittany stared up at him, desperately searching out the silver-gray lights in his eyes. She'd wanted to believe, so desperately. And now, of course, she could. She smiled, lowering her head.

"After tonight—you still want to marry me?"

"More than ever." He smiled and touched a lock of her tangled hair. "That fire in your hair is all a part of you, a part that I love with all my heart. No matter what, you were going to fight me. When you knew you would lose, you fought me anyway—"

"I thought you were a crook!"

"I know."

"Oh, Flynn!"

Brittany threw her arms around his neck and stood on tiptoe to capture his lips in a long and ardent kiss and when she came down to earth again, she was smiling up at him.

"You really love me. I mean—love me. Forever."

"I adore you," he whispered in return. "Forever."

"Oh, Flynn," she repeated, and this time he leaned to her, and their kiss was long and ardent and they couldn't come close enough together beneath the velvet sky.

Flynn sighed and rested his cheek against her head. "Let's go home, now, shall we."

"Home," she murmured. "Flynn, where is home going to be?"

"A castle in the uplands, the sand on Cocoa Beach, a flat in London, an apartment in New York. Will it really matter what we decide?"

She leaned against him, smiling.

"It won't matter at all, Flynn."

EPILOGUE

Flynn paused in his labors with the rigging and stared southeasterly, smiling. There was something about the view that
had called him; nature held him there in a bit of awe. He had
been called by her tune as any man might, and, as was a bit
unusual for him, he felt a touch of magic in the view.

It was a beautiful day; warm and balmy, but touched by
breezes. The ocean was at its shimmering best. To the south
and the east, deeper waters were gleaming indigo against the
clear horizon; here, the indigo paled to turquoise and green,
glittering, dancing, filling the senses with the varying mood of
the sea. Salt-clean and fresh, fantastic beneath the sun. The
sun . . . yes, today was one of those occasions that gave credence to the land mass behind them. Costa del Sol: coast of
the sun. Today belonged to the sea, and to the golden orb of
the fiery sun. To Neptune, and to all the various gods of the
seas.

To mermaids . . .

His own.

She was out there, on a small float, lazy, seductive, a sun
worshipper. Red hair drying in the breeze like a siren's bea-
con, limbs stretched out luxuriously, tanned and sultry.

He paused for a minute, thinking to leave her in that lazy,
lethargic peace.

Then he shrugged.

He left the rigging, cast the anchor, and returned to the rail, diving from it. Quick, strong strokes brought him to the float where a streak of pure mischief caused him to plummet beneath, cast the float over, and send her screeching and sputtering into the cool water beneath it.

Wet, laughing, she emerged, eyeing him warily from her side of the float, keeping a safe distance from him.

"You do know who you're dealing with here!" She warned him impertinently. "One who believes in an eye for an eye, a tooth for a tooth—a severe drenching for a severe drenching. And I can see by that smug grin upon your face, Mr. Colby, that you're thinking that you're twice my size and that I shall never get you under. But you're entirely wrong. I have patience. I shall wait, and when your mind is completely at rest and you're totally relaxed . . . then I will strike!"

Flynn laughed and edged around the float, breeching the distance between them.

"Perhaps, one day, it will happen. But not today." He leaned back and with a kick and a long crawl began to tow the float and Brittany toward the *Bella Christa*. "And actually, that was only justice you know, Brittany. The first time I dove into the water after you it was on a panicked rescue mission— and you were just fine. Such a wonderful little actress. Opening those emerald gems to me in such surprise . . ."

Brittany smiled secretively and lazily crawled back upon the float while he towed her. "Well, I was surprised, you know. I opened my eyes and knew instantly that I was out of my league."

"You weren't out of your league. You simply weren't playing with a full hand, my dear mermaid."

"I simply wasn't expecting you to be a pirate."

"Mmm . . ." Flynn murmured. He'd reached the yacht.

184

He tied a tow line to the float and tugged at it again, smiling as Brittany toppled off.

"Really . . ." she protested indignantly.

But Flynn caught her hand, laughing, and urged her up the ladder, following close behind her. She turned to him quickly only to find herself in his arms. Arms that dripped from the sea and burned with heat of the sun and held her so closely that she trembled, responding with an equal heat, her body so attuned to his.

"Flynn . . . ?"

He really had beautiful eyes. Blue and silver and gray and ever changing against the dark bronze of his features and the wet jet coloring of his hair.

"That first day," he told her huskily, "we were talking. Juan and I, you know. About Neptune and mermaids and nonsense. And then there you were. This mysterious, exotic beauty, cast up like a gift from the gods. Juan and I, being logical, had rather wondered what mortal man would do with a mermaid. I mean, what does one do with a fin?"

"You and Juan!" Brittany retorted. "I can well imagine!"

He laughed. "Well, pirates are supposed to be lusty fellows, you know."

"If you're going to play the role . . . ?"

"Precisely. I'm ever so glad that you came with long shapely mortal legs."

"And I'm ever so glad that you were a jealous pirate."

"Jealous?"

"If you hadn't chased me down at Ian's . . ."

He arched a brow to her. She found herself off of her feet and in his arms and they came into the cabin with the beautiful Victorian furniture and down on the sofa.

"Flynn, the furniture—"

"The hell with the furniture," he said fiercely. She saw that he wasn't so much teasing anymore, that he was tense, strained. He knelt beside her, watching her. "You told me that you wanted me," he reminded her, and she smiled, bringing her hand to his cheek.

"I did," she whispered. "But I'd have never made the first move. You were still on my suspect list, you know. And beyond that, I was afraid of your reputation. I did want you. That's why I'm glad that you were rotten and ill-tempered and jealous, otherwise, I'd have never been in the right position—"

"Oh," he murmured. "Rotten and ill-tempered and jealous?"

"Definitely."

"And you were all sweetness and innocence?"

"Much closer to it!" she defended herself.

She drew her finger from his cheek to the pulse at his throat, then gripped his shoulders and pulled herself toward him, placing a hot kiss against that pulse. She brought her hands down against his chest slowly, playing with the hair that grew there, following her touch with her kiss.

She felt his breath catch. She moved her hands lower and brought her fingers just beneath the waistband of his trunks and moved them slowly and erotically back and forth, just brushing his flesh.

He caught her hands.

"That's not exactly sweet and innocent behavior."

"No? Well I'm a quick study," she assured him, freeing her hands. She took the longest time to actually unbutton and unzip his cutoffs.

And he took a frightfully small amount of time to find the straps of her bikini, and free that meager fabric from her body. He pressed her back against the sofa and his mouth roamed hungrily over her until she ached.

186

"You taste like salt and sea . . . like a mermaid, Mrs. Colby," he told her. And he came between her thighs. Brittany gasped softly and shuddered and wound her legs welcomingly around him, closing her eyes slightly with the sensation of being loved and filled with desire when he entered her. Loving her . . .

"A mermaid," she said agreeably.

"With the most beautiful legs."

"Thank God."

"Oh, yes, thank God."

Later, much later, Brittany hugged a robe and came out to the deck and saw that Flynn was staring toward the sea again. He sensed that she was behind him. He reached out an arm and she came to him, situated happily in the shelter of his arms, leaned against his chest.

"We've got to get back in, you know," he murmured. "I wish we could stay forever. When I looked out and saw you on that float today, it was a little bit like magic all over again. That first day, I wanted you. And today . . . I have you."

"We can come back," she reminded him.

"We will come back." He set his chin upon her hand. They'd been married three weeks. This was honeymoon time. Special time. Tonight he'd be standing as best man for Juan— he and Rosa had been so taken with wedding fever that they had actually set a date for their own nuptials.

And in two days they had to be back in London, where Flynn was taking a more conservative position. And where Ian would be standing trial soon.

Flynn hugged Brittany closer to him. "Are you going to be all right?"

She knew exactly what he was talking about. She nodded. "I'm going to be fine."

"I'm only sorry that we met through Alice's death," Flynn said softly.

Brittany turned in his arms to face him earnestly. "She would have loved you. And I think that she'd be very, very happy with this outcome."

Flynn smiled and drew her hands to him, kissing her fingertips.

"So soon," Brittany murmured.

"Mmm."

"We have to get back."

"Mmm."

"We should come here every year."

"Mmm."

"It's so special."

He picked up his wrist, glancing at his sports watch. "Mmm."

"Flynn, you're not listening—"

"Oh, but I am!" Laughing, he tugged at her robe, leading her back to the cabin. "So soon, have to go back—magical beings and special cases. Well, we do have to go back. And my love, this particular pirate doesn't care to waste one glorious moment of that time, and so my leggy mermaid, if you've no objections . . ."

Brittany lowered her lashes, amazed that she could still blush.

"Well . . . ?"

She didn't answer him. She smiled sweetly and cast her robe on deck. Her hair cascaded down her naked back, and for a moment she might have appeared as a flaming sea goddess.

"Flynn . . ."

"Yes?"

"Aunt Alice would have been very happy, you know. I acquired not only a husband, but . . ."

"But?"

"Another living blood relation. Well, soon, at any rate."

She turned then, and headed for the cabin.

"Brittany, what? Brittany—wait! Brittany, what—"

He paused, feeling a vast flood of emotion warm him, shudder through him. "Brittany . . . ?"

He grinned, cast his robe aside, and followed her in.